The Vision
And Beyond

The Vision
And Beyond

Maggie Shaw

eregendal.com

First published in the United Kingdom in 2018,
eregendal.com, Crewe, Cheshire.
Printed in the United Kingdom by Lulu.com.

ISBN 978-1-9996071-0-4 (paperback)

INTRODUCTION
AND ACKNOWLEDGEMENTS

The Vision and Beyond is a mystical story, in the style of the novels of Charles Williams. Its Cold War setting adds to the atmosphere of foreboding which permeates the work. The literary device that no landmark is named is deliberate. The story explores betrayal, healing, faith and identity as it unravels two mysteries. The first is to discover the real name of the woman at the centre of the story. The second is to find out what happened to the world during the woman's three-year imprisonment.

The book was inspired by a chance comment from a friend in the late 1970s about neutron bombs destroying people but not property. It has developed over the years since, thanks in no small part to the wisdom and advice of many people, including Rev. Angus Logan, Rev. John Woolcock, and Rev. Edward Robertson. I would also like to thank Tonya Chirgwin, Lynn Rose and Roy Butler for their assistance with the manuscript, and Helen Lamb for her help with the artwork and cover design. Any faults in the work are my own alone.

The Biblical passage from Micah on page 65 is quoted from the New Revised Standard Version of the Bible. Other Biblical quotations are from the King James Version. The song words quoted on page 98 are from the tango *Hernando's Hideaway*, written by Jerry Ross and Richard Adler, from the musical *The Pajama Game*, first published in 1954.

Part 1

Into The Vision……

CHAPTER 1

The early spring morning was grey with drizzle. A lingering mist drifted over the slow waters of the broad river and through the bleak woods along the banks, softening the skeletal outlines of the budding ash and birch trees. The river was spanned by a makeshift wood and steel bridge built onto the squat stone pillars of a much earlier construction. Its metal parapets were defended with rolls of barbed wire, and at each end stood a black and yellow sentry box beside a single-bar gate.

A small black car arrived at the gate on the south bank and parked to block off the southern approach to the bridge. A large man alighted. He exchanged a few brief words with the khaki-clad sentry who had challenged him from the box, and returned to the car to wait.

Ten minutes later a cortege of large black cars came to a halt at the north gate. Two armed sentries clad in blue serge stepped out of their box to challenge the people in the leading car. After the reply, one of the sentries moved on to the second car to converse briefly with the passenger in the back seat. The sentry answered a question with an affirmative nod and a wave to the south gate, and then returned to his box. His colleague marched across the road to stand guard on the far side of the gate.

Three people emerged from the third car in the north-side cortege. Their breath condensed in the chilly air as they walked slowly towards the north gate. The sentries raised the gate for them to pass. One of the three led the way onto the bridge. The other two followed, walking closely together with the awkward gait of those who had no affinity but the handcuffs linking them. The sentries closed the gate again behind them. They stopped to wait on the north end of the bridge with their backs towards the gate.

On the south bank the large man re-emerged from the small black car. His left hand held a briefcase. The khaki-clad sentry raised the south gate and saluted him as he walked past onto the bridge, closing the gate behind him. He paused to light a cigarette. His wary eyes scanned the north bank, taking in every detail: the mist, the cortege of large black cars, the disposition of the tense men on the north bank, the gentle lapping of the sluggish water against the banks and the bridge stanchions; the cowed prisoner huddling in an ill-fitting raincoat, waiting fearfully for the moment of release. He paused for a few moments until his instinct told him it was safe to go ahead. When he walked across to the centre of the bridge his footsteps thudded on the wood beneath, their echo deadened by the mist.

He stopped abruptly, watching the people in front of the north gate as he drew sharply on his cigarette. They did not move. He threw the half-smoked stub over the parapet into the river and set down the black brief-case in front of him. Still there was no movement along the river banks. He slipped his hands into his coat pockets and strolled back to the south gate. There he stopped and turned to watch.

The leader of the three people at the north gate stepped out onto the bridge. He crouched down beside the brief-case and inspected the contents with large deliberate movements to show that he was attempting no tricks. The papers he saw inside met with his approval. He closed the case with a nod and walked away from it back to the north gate to send on the two people waiting there. As they crossed together to the centre of the bridge, he too turned to watch.

The couple halted by the briefcase. The captor unlocked the handcuffs and set his captive free. Using the empty cuff, he chained the briefcase to his wrist and hurried back to the north gate. The blue-uniformed sentries quickly readmitted him and his colleague to the river bank and opened the passenger doors of the third black car for them to get back in.

The liberated captive paused for a moment on the bridge and gazed apprehensively over the parapet at the river banks beyond. That was the moment when the shots should ring out to end the charade. But no shots sounded. Nothing stirred in the undergrowth beneath the gaunt trees. The freedom of that exchange was not to be the release of convenient death.

On such a significant day every detail of that fresh early spring morning stood out to the captive as though in sharp relief: the misty greys of the river beneath and the wooded banks against the heavy sky; the haunting call of a hawk scaring its prey into flight as it wheeled in the air on the hunt; the lapping of the water against the ancient stanchions of the damaged bridge.

The large man was still waiting at the south gate, his face expressionless. The captive took one last longing look at freedom and walked on across the bridge into his custody. The gate was raised to admit them onto the south bank. They climbed into the small car and drove away.

The cortege on the north bank departed immediately after, the political exchange effectively complete.

CHAPTER 2

The large man drove the small black car in a south-westerly direction. He opened a packet of cigarettes and offered one to his prisoner, hoping that his show of friendship would tempt her to discard her defences; the hood of her raincoat, her silence, her stern looks; but she said nothing. She did not move.

'Smoke, Katy?' he prompted.

His invitation was carefully non-committal in tone, neither aggressive nor sympathetic. It conveyed a certain impartial amiability to her which touched the right chord in her memory. She took a cigarette from the packet. He noted that her hand shook.

'Who are you?' she ventured, her mezzo-contralto voice low with apprehension. Her accent was that of an educated homelander, with some faint traces of a northern dialect.

'To you I am no-one. Call me what you like,' he said.

'Okay, Smith: Mr Smith!' she spat.

Her contemptuous inflexion failed to disturb him. He noted her bitterness without rancour because he understood the circumstances which had made her react so defiantly. He was confident that he had the advantage: she would have to be far more responsive if she wanted her cigarette to be lit. He drove on in silence through the wooded countryside, waiting for her to relent. After a while he realised that he would need to prompt her again.

'Not very friendly, are we.'

'After those bastards? You expect me to be friendly? They have taught me there are only bastards in this world!'

Her outburst amused him though he took care not to show it. In his experience such misguided defiance only concealed the fear of people who did not know what they were playing with.

'Not very friendly at all, considering all the trouble I took to secure your release.'

'You will have your reasons. Why did you bother?'

'I'll come to that later. After three years your story will not spoil for a few hours more.'

'You paid a big enough price for me. I heard what the documents were in that case.'

'Those? They are nothing. They were not paying your price.'

She turned sharply to look at him from out of the depths of her hood. His dismissive reply gave her the impression of having been discarded or thrown out rather than released.

'What do you mean?' she demanded: 'Who are you? And who do you represent?'

'No-one you would know.'

'No? Try me.'

He ignored her challenge and drove on in silence through the misty countryside. The unlit cigarette was still resting in her right hand. He wondered whether she had learnt to treat cigarettes as a form of currency during her imprisonment and was mistakenly trying to keep hold of it to barter with later. She tried to ignore his presence and stared through the windscreen at the changing landscape. After a lengthy journey she realised where they were going.

'Why are you taking me to the capital, Mr Smith?' she demanded.

'You need to recuperate after your ordeal. I am taking you to the best hotel I know that's still standing, so that you can do just that.'

She drew back her hood in a wordless acknowledgement that his patience was beginning to earn a little of her trust. Her face was gaunt and large-featured, unsoftened by the rough cut of her short dark brown hair; physical indications of the privative regime she had endured. Her dark liquid eyes conveyed a tragic sorrow which belied the bitter defiance she voiced, showing it to be no more than a barrier to keep the world at a distance and him at bay.

'I do not like hotels, however good. Nor do I care for capitals,' she declared.

'Maybe, but this one's different: they had to evacuate it two years ago. Your fellow compatriots succeeded without your help, as you will no doubt have heard.'

'I have heard nothing. I have seen no-one. Only soldiers. Pah!'

He sighed to hear her contempt. If she continued to resist his offers of friendship and still refused to speak, he would have to use other methods to make her talk. He retrieved a box of matches from his coat pocket and threw them on the dashboard. She thanked him with a sullen mutter and lit her cigarette, casually trying afterwards to pocket the matches. He had been expecting that prison trick and held out his left hand for their return. She begrudgingly placed the box in his hand. He returned the matches to his pocket without comment.

'Anyone you want to contact now you're free?' he enquired.

The question was a trap, she realised.

'Am I free?' she returned.

She looked at him for a reaction but he appeared not to have heard her. Through her thoughts passed images of people she thought she used to know. As each face passed she imagined what might happen should she make contact while he lurked in the background.

'No,' she replied at length, 'there is no-one I wish to contact.'

'Good, good,' he bluffed with false bonhomie: 'All the better for us; and for you too, indirectly.'

She eyed him with a penetrating stare but found to her surprise that she could not see through him in the way she could most people. He had obscured his identity in her alternative vision with a veil far denser than the mist shrouding the countryside around them, making her unable to gauge the manner of his bluff.

'But there will be people who would want to contact me,' she said uneasily.

He almost smiled. Her defensive response told him that she did want to contact some people and if caught doing so would claim that they were the ones who had initiated such contact. He still needed her alone and helpless. He deliberately dismissed their involvement with a reassuring comment to keep her solely dependent on himself.

'You needn't worry about them, Katy: we have already taken adequate precautions to prevent their interference.'

'We? Who is this "we"?' she demanded.

'Don't expect me to answer that. I just follow orders. That's my job.'

'Really? Then what is mine?'

'To rest and recuperate,' he reassured with bright geniality.

'In the best hotel you could requisition? It seems I am a prisoner still.'

Her voice had an edge of sorrow. To while away the long hours in prison she had often dreamed of all the things she would do when she was finally free again: rambling along leafy lanes through fields of ripening corn, and running along the beach with some dogs at low tide; huddling by the fire in a cottage while a winter gale raged outside, and gratefully consigning herself to the mundane routine of work; and learning to cook all those dishes she had visualised while she had eaten the meagre prison food. And here she was back in her homeland with her papers in her pocket; but instead of doing those things and a thousand others like them, she was being driven by this secretive stranger to a gilded cage no less imprisoning than those previous cells, for all its greater comfort.

'Will I ever be free?' she asked.

Tears began to prick her eyes. She choked back a sob in surprise: she had been through so much she sometimes believed she had forgotten how to cry. She brought her emotions back under control before she softly added,

'I mean, truly free: free to go home and start living again.'

He was unmoved by her swimming eyes and her choking voice, and dismissed her question impatiently.

'You threw that away yourself, when you crossed the border three years ago!'

She turned to him in dismay.

'Me? I threw it away?' she repeated. 'O Smith, how wrong you are!'

CHAPTER 3

The city wept. Once so impressive in its evening greys, now its rain-washed façade was drab and decayed. It cried out for the brightening touch of colour and the enlivening breath of humanity, with blank windows that stared darkly on black tarmac, and white stone streaked with weathered droppings and smoke stains. The clouds reflected the capital's grief and mourned in sympathy over the marks of its desertion: the empty littered streets and pillaged shops, the silenced cathedrals and the stilled factories. Across the grimy remnants of the unseen advertising hoardings, faded messages still lay in wait to stir an absent populace into purchasing unmarketed products. In more hidden corners, on pitted brick and concrete, eroded graffiti mouthed silent dirges to the originators of insults long since gone. Carved into the trunks of leafless trees, hearts and arrows made a material denial of the transient reality of love. Yearning for its makers and the occupants who had once given it purpose, the city wept tears of crumbling stone and brick into empty thoroughfares which once had thronged with traffic, and quiet alleys where children once had played, and at the weathered feet of statuary angels placed as witnesses for posterity who could only cover their averted sightless eyes with pitted unbending wings. The atomic clock in the heart of the city alone lived on without faltering, its mindless programmed precision continuing whether or not humanity still existed to give its purpose meaning. What did such a clock's precision mean to the captive who gazed from her hotel balcony across the evening city but could not see its ever-changing moon-shaped face?

She turned, drink in hand, to stroll back into the plush green lounge of her seventh-floor suite. As she stepped through the lace-curtained patio doors and down the two carpeted steps inside, she also stepped back in dismay through that old familiar edge of darkness into the potentially infinite void of her spiritual shadowland. There her soul revolved like a golden helix on an invisible thread and cried out against vacuity in its desperate attempt to find identity and purpose. That nameless quality of existence which permeated her world with its tangible *I am*, fled from her grasp when she tried to look at it more closely. Philosophy had departed with Smith, as had her name; and religion had long since abandoned her, a dangerous vehicle whose glossy black body shell encased the polluting engine of science to convey the corrupt machinations of the driver at its wheel. She stood alone, a solitary captive in a fallen city with a drink in her hand and a cigarette in her mouth, three things she had once despised for their pollution. And still the golden helix revolved in the dark void of depression, its invisible thread somehow still intact despite all the agony of that nightmare past.

How she had longed during those three years to return to the land of her birth; but this was not the homecoming she had longed for or expected or even once by chance imagined. From beyond the patio doors she could hear the blind buildings calling to her with haunting voices which all told their own harrowing tales. She slammed the windows shut to keep out their cries and threw the heavy green curtains across to hide their faces, distraught with their sorrow. To her relief her actions deadened the volume of their voices and cut out the penetrating trebles of their cries from the lounge, leaving only a thin trace of their message to reverberate distantly in the muffled hum of some forgotten traffic jam.

She sat back down and poured herself another drink. Oblivion tempted her to leave her hell from hell, if only for a couple of hours, but even as she sipped her second glass her conscience reminded her she would find no escape through crawling inside a wine bottle. She set the glass down on the low table in front of her and wondered about the past for giving her such a conscience. There seemed to be no justification for such caution amongst what she could still recall of her experience. This was no surprise. Ever since she had endured solitary confinement, she had found that life had become like a dream, unsubstantial and without logic, whenever no-one else was there for her to relate to as a person. Now, for instance, she could feel eddies of unsuspected happenings stirring the air of the city around her; but she had shut the city out. She allowed logic to overrule intuition and reasoned that the air could only be being stirred by herself, as the golden helix of her soul spun on its thin invisible thread in an infinite void which felt like endless night.

Only the material world could combat such spiritual dissociation. She reached out her right hand to the low table in front of her and grasped hold of its smooth chrome-framed glass top. Its unbending cold substance shocked her senses and surprised her mind back into her body. Alone she was, as always; a prisoner she was, as always; but that did not allow her to relax the self-discipline which kept her mind, her body and her soul corded together; despite the unsubstantial worlds which always tempted her at her weakest times to relinquish her hold on the material world and escape through the barred windows to the golden universes which she knew lay somewhere beyond.

Doors. She turned to the doors. She tried every door in the suite: bedroom, bathroom, cabinets, wardrobes. Only one door would not open to her, the one door she needed to be open. She went to bed and slept, hoping that the door to freedom would have opened of its own accord before the morning. Sleep was blessed with dreams of the secure little cell where she had spent the last weeks of her imprisonment, the place where she had begun to learn that the opening of the door was not always something to dread.

She awoke early next morning greatly refreshed by her sleep and able to face any challenge with confidence. She spent some time in bed simply enjoying the luxury of her pink and grey hotel bedroom before she moved herself to get up. When she went to the bathroom to shower she found a new set of clothes laid out for her. She hunted for her old clothes but could not find them. Her few possessions had been placed neatly on the dressing table in the bedroom. Her papers were not among them.

She bridled at these physical reminders of her continuing captivity. With no papers she would risk her life in any attempt to escape; or perhaps her captors desired to take her life anyway and tried only to ensure that they could claim to have been provoked. She put on the new clothes and found greater resentment at being expected to wear military khaki for her third term, despite the green wool being warm and comfortably practical to wear. She had to remind herself that her appearance hardly mattered when no-one was around to take meaning from the design of her attire. She filed her few possessions in the pockets of the rough khaki jacket and strolled back out into the lounge.

On the glass-topped chrome table she found a breakfast tray which could only have been placed there while she was dressing after her shower. She ran to find the waiter, desperately opening doors, but found no-one: the one door he would have used, that same door that she longed to walk through, was still locked. She gave up her search as abruptly as she had started it and sat down by the glass-topped table to break her fast.

As she was finishing the last slice of toast she realised that the wall stand, which she had been staring intently at during the meal, was supporting a radio which she could not remember being there before. She left her food at once and switched the radio on, but picked up only static as she turned the tuner through the wavelengths. She returned to her breakfast in renewed disappointment.

After she had sat back down she noticed a packet of cigarettes on the breakfast tray. She had not seen the cigarettes on the tray before, yet they were leaning against the coffee pot from which she had already poured a cup; and she was certain that no-one had entered the room to place the packet there while her attention was taken up with the radio.

The old panic began to rise in her again. Such inconsistencies in what her senses perceived were often a warning of insanity. Her perceptual problem lay in the mysterious appearances and changes of everyday objects around her. In the absence of any plausible logical explanation for this she decided to accept such happenings as expressions of a so far undefined phenomenon of the new life in her changed homeland. Though the solution was meaningless beyond being a play with concept, it did at least allow her to ignore the incidents before they unnerved her completely. The device stopped them being miracles and left them as mere events whose causality would probably become manifest later.

She threw back the curtains and flung open the patio doors to readmit the sounds of the deserted city. The tired buildings outside were softly recalling a dawn chorus of sparrow song and traffic noise from the deserted park and the empty streets. Its audience of one felt moved by the poignant prelude to grieve its grief for the mortal makers who through death had forgotten their city, and for the absent parents who had turned their backs to avert their eyes from the desolation and had deafened their ears to the cries in their shame and guilt for the fate of their capital. She spoke to the city with words of consolation, conscious of the way her breath disturbed the stillness of the early morning air, and the way her soft voice drowned out the whispers from the walls. Yet for all her compassion she had to admit that this was how she liked the capital most, because for once the memories it recalled in the stone tape were not drowned out by the noises of today.

The atomic clock struck seven. The city fell silent. The air crispened into the tense atmosphere of a concert hall when the orchestra is under the conductor's baton and the performance is about to start. The audience of one leaned forward expectantly on her feet in her box on the hotel balcony, and waited with her full attention for the symphony to begin.

The opening notes were almost imperceptible, like the whispered majesty of the opening bars of the symphony which a modern homeland composer had written to this capital more than eighty years before its fall. The gentle murmur of distant diesel engines moved gradually closer through the streets with a passive bass statement of the leit-motif which was quickly taken up by the more powerful tenor of massing petrol engines. These in their turn were augmented by the strong contralto voice of weaving motorcycles, until the soprano descant of the horns brought the extended crescendo of the first movement into a sustained climax of vehicles passing beneath the balcony, half gliding smoothly by, half stopping and starting in staccato emphasis. The climax reached a deafening fortissimo, before retreating through a gradual diminuendo back to a murmur before the close.

The second movement began at once with a blast from what sounded like an overpoweringly loud cannon. This was followed by the crash of falling masonry punctuated with other blasts and crashes, and sirens and alarm bells. Through their dying discords advanced the threatening beat of military drums and the measured footsteps of disciplined forces marching through the streets. Behind the dominant beat, weak voices shouted protests and light footfalls fled away. Authoritarian voices gave orders through loud hailers for the streets to be evacuated and the hospitals to be closed and the night-time curfew to be punishable by death. Gunshots rattled out. The footfalls died away. The streets fell silent.

After a significant pause the largo movement began. The city wept its masonry tears to cover the open graves of the unseen multitude who had perished there in its midst, and to mourn its makers who had departed never to return. The largo was formless, seemingly endless: its audience looked down in compassion on the empty streets waiting for its conclusion so that the fourth movement could begin and the symphony be brought to its finale. But then the captive realised that the fourth movement had not yet happened, that the concluding events in the destruction of the capital had not yet been enacted for its levelling or its reprieve. Under no illusions about the negligible part she would play in that final movement, she wept tears for the sufferings borne by this once mighty edifice in world affairs: only tears could be accorded to such a controlled rendition of intense tragedy. Who would remember that tragedy the longer, she wondered, humanity or its crumbling monument the dying city? Swiftly her subconscious brought the clear answer from its depths as the city fell silent: the world itself would remember, for in the Akashic Record no memory, however trivial the incident or thought, would ever fade away.

She looked up to the sun, which was now high in the sky and shining on the land with a spring warmth which did not permeate the shadows. The sun had also witnessed the tragedy that had inspired that momentous symphony from the streets below; but the unblinking sun gave no sign: it had its own destiny to fulfil and was not required to consider its dependents in its deeds. Like its spark within the atomic clock in the heart of the city, the sun continued in its task to follow its course whether or not it was being observed. And she too was required to do so by creation, as she had discovered while confined in solitary, for she had still continued to exist even when she was not being considered by others. But why had she not died then, the voice inside her asked: why had the invisible thread not broken when the golden helix no longer spun; and where had she learnt to read the Akashic Record or even heard of its name; and who else read the Akashic Record, for a document was only compiled and kept when it was required, and more than she was in that document. Was she being observed by some greater being whom she did not know, but who had saved her from no longer existing when she was no longer considered by men?

She sighed at such unanswerable questions and returned to the lounge, deliberately using physical activity to take the place of the philosophic uncertainties in her mind. She found that her breakfast tray had been taken away and the radio placed in its stead on the glass-topped table. Hoping that there might be some significance to this, she sat back down at the table and tried again to tune the radio in to a broadcasting station. Again she picked up only static; until her hand slipped on the dial and the tuner by chance picked up a mayday message from a ship foundering at sea. She turned the radio off in anguish, acutely conscious of her own inability to help. She could only hope that someone somewhere in the world was in a position to send aid; and even that not for the best of reasons: she desired the ship to be saved because if the crew survived she might be able to meet up with them and escape her living hell.

Then she looked up, and saw that the door was open.

CHAPTER 4

She ran towards the door, but stopped in sudden fear. Her hand was on the lintel, her right foot on the brink. The corridor in front of her was in darkness: anything might be hiding in its shadows; Smith with a gun, perhaps, or ghosts of the past, or something less definable but more evil. She turned back to the suite, and faltered again, this time with astonishment rather than fear.

The lounge was bare. She stepped apprehensively onto the rough white floorboards. Her cautious footsteps resounded on the wood and reverberated around the stripped walls. Dumfounded by the dramatic and unprecedented change in the room, she sat down cross-legged in the centre of the floor and lit up a cigarette as she tried to understand what had happened.

The smoke from the cigarette drifted gently in the air and threw a mist over her mind. She could feel its lethargic effects creeping through her body and realised that it was not helping her to face her problem at all. It merely took away her drive and smoothed the edges of her fear, subtly offering her an escape through a form of oblivion which would only prove to be another form of suicide. But even suicide had its attractions while she was yet a captive. She pulled her eyes away from the unexpected temptation of the balcony and returned her thoughts to the enigma of the stripped room.

She had had a dream once in her sleep where she had faced this sort of reality. The dream had been so vivid that she had later asked a knowledgeable friend whether such a thing could happen in reality. She could still see his amused face as he replied that in science nothing was impossible, but many things were unlikely. From that she now drew the conclusion that although the disappearance of the entire furnishings of a room without noise or trace in only five seconds was unlikely, it was not impossible. It was disconcerting, of course; but life was disconcerting, and many other things as strange as this had happened to her since her first time in solitary. She had placed those incidents on the top shelf in her mind until their explanation turned up, having learnt that her mental stability was placed at far less risk if she meanwhile ignored them. There was no need to handle this event any differently, beyond taking it as a warning to expect further bizarre happenings. Her homeland had clearly changed, and existence itself had apparently changed too, for several of its new natural laws were far removed from the former logical rules and powers by which she and all creation had lived before.

She resolved to let nothing disconcert her and to accept all things as they proved themselves to be however illogical their appearance or lack of explanation might seem. Her mind settled, she stood up again, trod out her cigarette on the floorboards, and turned back towards the door. It was shut.

A footfall from the bathroom made her spin back round in alarm. Smith strolled out, thickset in a beige raincoat. His face was impassive beneath the brim of his trilby hat.

'Why didn't you take the chance while it was there? Now I'll have to ask you some questions,' he said.

She did not answer. With a chilling look of hatred she turned back to try the handle of the door. It was locked, as his question had implied it would be. Her fingers gripped the handle fiercely, her disappointment too great for her to let him see her face. She silently cursed the fear which had made her turn her back on freedom when only one step further would have meant escape.

'I didn't want to question you,' Smith continued: 'That's why I gave you the chance to go. You've forced my hand. I'm sorry.'

His apology did not convince her. She turned back to face him, massaging her hand which had grown stiff with grasping the door-handle too fiercely. He watched disinterestedly, knowing that she would be struggling to process the confusion his tactics had created. Her clarity of thought was greater than he imagined. She reminded herself that she did not have to answer any of his questions: she was not answerable to him or to anyone. After those months in solitary silence was an easy game to play.

'What made you go over to the other side three years ago?' he asked.

He opened the uncurtained patio doors. Before she had a chance to answer his question he strolled out onto the balcony, clearly not bothered about hearing her reply. Her astonishment at his lack of interest totally eclipsed her indignation at the phrasing of his question. She choked back a heated explanation that the route of the minibus holiday tour had passed through several countries, not just gone directly to the other side. The pause reminded her of her intention to keep silent. She sneered at Smith behind his broad rounded back for his inability to force her to reply.

He smiled inwardly as he gazed across the park. Now her silence was playing right into his hands. Already he was stringing phrases together for his report: she had failed to answer his questions adequately; no, she had proved so resistant to interrogation that, the only course of action she left open to him was to allow her to escape and see who she ran to.

'Why did they imprison you?' he asked.

He turned and leaned back against the balcony rail to look at her. She hastily dropped her sneer but sensed that he had detected her contempt and had construed an answer from her silence. She could not give an answer to his new question because she did not know the answer herself. To save having to admit this even to herself, she looked down at the whitewood floorboards and concentrated her thoughts on the rough-cut texture and the pattern of the grain.

Smith watched her patiently. He understood what she as yet

did not, that she needed to find herself again before she could answer anything with confidence. First he needed to persuade her to start looking, but because of her reactive prisoner mentality he would have to convince her that his intentions were quite different before he let her go and followed her to earth.

'The ceiling is more impressive,' he remarked.

She looked up automatically, hearing too late the insult in his patronising remark. With a sham look of modesty she dropped her gaze again to hide her mistake from him, though she did have to acknowledge to herself that his remark was correct.

The ceiling had become a delicate powder blue with ornate white plaster mouldings, where before its darker colour had been a delicate powder green. The cause of such an enigmatic change became clear to her at once in all its simplicity: a different room had been placed around her. She smiled at herself for not having recognised such a simple substitution before.

Smith saw her smile and strolled back into the bare room.

'Try to think of me as your friend, Katy,' he said: 'After all, you'll need all the friends you can get once the authorities get hold of you.'

'Why? Aren't you the authorities?' she demanded.

He shook his head and shrugged his shoulders with an enigmatic smile to give her a conflicted reply.

'Maybe, maybe not,' he said, compounding the conflict.

The subtlety of his device went over her head.

'What would the authorities want with me?' she scoffed without thought of his professional position.

'The same as I do, I presume. There again, you were a card-carrying member until you defected. They won't be very nice to you now you're back.'

'But I didn't defect! I only went on holiday, with some friends. And I wasn't a card-carrying member! That's the last thing I would have been.'

Her protest told him that his stratagem was working.

Knowing that few people can resist denying false questions when they are delivered with that quiet force which states the interrogator's facts are correct, he continued to goad her on.

'Went on holiday? And never came back? And crossing the border without a visa – being smuggled across?'

'That's not true!' she cried indignantly: 'The people organising the tour, they got the visas for us. And I never came back only 'cause I was....'

She faltered and hesitated, her mind unexpectedly blank.

'Was what, Katy?'

She turned aside, confused, unable to remember why she had not come back at the end of that holiday. She had been out of the country for three years, but she could only remember a fortnight of the three-week tour and a total of thirty months' imprisonment. Smith would hardly hear that from her and be convinced. She lit a cigarette and walked out onto the balcony to think.

The air outside was shimmering in the unusual warmth of the afternoon sun. Its distortion made the streets appear to be waving to her and beckoning her down to join them. Their invitation gave her an attractive alternative course of action to follow. She nodded her thanks to the deserted streets below and returned confidently to the stripped lounge.

'I am going for a walk, Smith,' she announced.

Her firm resolve did not trouble him: he had been playing the scene to chase her away. He stepped aside for her as she crossed the room to the door.

She threw out the doubts which told her the door to freedom would still be locked, and summoned instead that confidence of faith which knew it would open. She grasped the handle firmly and turned it. The door opened. She stepped outside into the corridor beyond.

CHAPTER 5

The long dark corridor stretched out in front of her like something from a childhood nightmare. As an eight-year-old she had not known what prize awaited her at the far end but had felt compelled to run through the twisting black tunnel to find out. Now she knew the goal she sought to reach, and because she also knew the tunnel might be endless she chose to walk.

Despite having no light to show her where to tread her footsteps along the stale thin carpet did not falter. She guided herself down the passage by reaching out her left hand and running her fingers lightly over the wall to keep her distance as she moved. Some sixty paces further on, she came to the end of the passage and a pair of swing doors. Beyond these she found an unlit stairwell of carpeted steps descending in an anti-clockwise direction. She placed her left hand on the central bannister and cautiously began a blind descent, carefully testing the edge and depth of each step with her toes before transferring her weight. The staircase pattern turned out to be a simple arrangement of flights of twelve steps which enabled her to speed up her descent.

Fourteen flights down she came to a dimly lit landing. Its only light shone in through two oblong reinforced-glass windows in a pair of swing doors which gave access to the ground floor. When she looked through one of the windows and saw where she was, she strolled out through the doors into the hotel lobby, feeling a great sense of achievement.

The lobby was a large vaulted hall with a dated appeal of tired and neglected opulence. Between the sturdy marble pillars, groups of grimy easy chairs and sofas gathered around dusty low tables, with backdrops of dead rubber plants and aspidistras in tarnished brass pots. At the long reception desk a waxwork concierge offered a plastic resident a gleaming key to room number X15. A wooden couple embraced in greeting nearby. On a couch bordering the aisle, a tailor's dummy dressed as a businessman sat primly reading a copy of a leading national newspaper. None of the people moved. All of them were frozen in unbecoming attitudes as though they had all been caught by chance in a still frame of a three-dimensional film.

She strolled across the foyer and sat down beside the businessman to look over his shoulder at his newspaper, hoping that it might tell her what had happened to her homeland. Although the paper appeared to be fresh from the press, the date she deciphered beneath the title made it about two years old. She glanced down at the front page, which appeared to be printed clearly until she looked at it more closely and found herself unable to read any of the articles or identify anyone in the photographs. The juxtaposition of letters in words and dots in images made nonsense of the content. She wondered whether the jumbled words were anagrammatic and looked again at one of the headlines. Then she remembered Smith upstairs and warned herself not to waste her time there fruitlessly.

She moved on to find a working telephone and tried the one on the reception desk. As she lifted the handset the dialing tone purred in her ear. She turned her back to the leering waxwork concierge with the gleaming key for the plastic guest, and dialed a number which had just come into her head. She associated the number with a friend who had once lived in the city, and hoped that help might be forthcoming there. The number proved to be unobtainable.

A hand seemed to tap her lightly on the shoulder. She looked back in surprise at the plastic guest behind her, but he did not appear to have moved. She shrugged her shoulders and turned back to the telephone.

The next number she recalled and tried was that of an aunt who used to live in the countryside beyond the suburbs. That also proved to be unobtainable. Wondering whether she was wasting her effort, she tried the number of her parents' house in the outer suburbs: if anyone was still alive, they would be, she thought with a wry smile. Her third call connected, but rang out unanswered.

Again she felt as though someone had tapped her on the shoulder. She turned to stare more crossly at the plastic guest, and thought she recognised the clothes he was wearing, though she could not place him. The gleaming key he was about to take stood out suddenly as a key to understanding, but at that moment and with the little information she had found out so far, she could not tell what mystery that key should unlock.

Remembered phone numbers began to flood into her thoughts. She tried one with an exchange number in one of the northern counties, hoping the place would be so far removed from city civilisation that whatever might have happened in the capital, it was still likely to be carrying on as normal. Her call was connected by a tired automatic exchange system. After four rings an answering machine clicked on.

'Fairfield Commune. No-one is available at the moment. Please wait for the tone, then leave your message and a number for us to call you back.'

She panicked and slammed down the receiver. Though she recognised the voice, the name of the farm was wrong. The friend who had married and moved north there with her new husband some years before, had started a new life on their own farm, not a commune. Had they been evicted and turned back into tenants by predatory reformers, she wondered, or had the rest of the country also suffered dramatic changes during the destruction of the capital?

A hand tapped her shoulder a third time. There was no mistaking it; and with it she heard the voice of a young man she had got to know three years ago, now whispering an urgent command for her to get out of the hotel. Fear flooded her senses. She turned in panic and ran towards the bank of rotating doors leading to the outside world. Above, the building trembled and groaned. She dived through the right-hand door. It spun more rapidly than she expected and catapulted her out into the deserted street.

Behind her, the building gave one last mighty groan and collapsed, falling inward on itself. Chunks of concrete, fragments of glass and other debris flew up into the air and rained down on the streets. Dust rose in choking clouds which swirled and settled on everything around. Crash upon crash reverberated around the impenetrable facades of the tall buildings nearby.

For a moment it felt to her as though the end of the world had come. She crouched where she had landed in the street, with her arms over her head for protection, hoping that after everything she had been through, she would be allowed to survive this. Gradually the commotion died down around her and she knew the worst was past. She rolled over into a seated position and coughed heartily amid the settling dust.

The city fell silent. It seemed to be paying its last respects with her to the building which had just died in its midst. All that remained of the hotel was a huge pile of rubble and the bank of revolving doors, still intact in their glazed wooden frame, all three spinning rapidly still as though to shake out the human presence which had fled through them to escape the hotel's fall.

She picked herself up off the ground and walked stiffly away, still shaking after her close shave. She wondered whether Smith had also survived the collapse of the building: if he had not, she had just lost the only person she had talked to in her homeland since her return. She wondered whether Smith had known beforehand about the dangerous state of the hotel: if he had, he was playing a particularly nasty game of cat and mouse with her which would place him in the same league as her jailors on the other side. But all those considerations were at worst. At best, she was free.

Her footsteps became more confident, her head higher, her back more straight. Even the stone-strewn pavement seemed to reach up to her feet to welcome her there. The flagstones told her how glad they felt to be trodden once more by human footsteps after two lonely years of waiting for the absent ones to return. Shattered shop windows leaned out their plundered displays to her, hungry for her glance, desperate for her approval of their wares, lusting for her entrance through their doors.

At first she pretended not to be interested. She deliberately ignored their licentious soliciting, cruelly playing on their vulnerable loneliness. Such sadism was not natural to her. Her occasional hardness was only an after-effect of recent events, superimposed upon an amiable personality which always re-emerged to urge her to relent. A shoe shop caught her attention. For some reason she had long had a fascination for shoes. She turned aside to gaze through the undamaged window at the colourful and varied display of brogues and sandals, boots and slippers. Even to have stopped her meant the shop had won. She pushed open the door and walked inside.

The interior of the shop was dim, the only light coming in through the windows. She scratched around in the gloom, looking for a matching pair of shoes in her size that appealed to her sense of taste and occasion. The neat wall racks on the sales floor displayed only right shoes. In the store-room at the back of the shop the corresponding left shoes and their boxes lay in heaps on the floor where they had been emptied off the shelves. At length she managed to pair up two suede laced ankle boots which felt comfortable enough for walking distances. She threw her stout army shoes in a large green canvas shoulder bag which she picked out from a rack near the door, and walked back out into the street feeling more confident for being differently shod. The shop sent her on her way with a blessing for her custom, glad to give her the articles to show its appreciation of her approval and the advertising she would generate: perhaps through her visit the next customer would be less than two years away.

After replacing her shoes, she next wanted to replace her

unappealing army uniform. She turned a corner looking for a clothes shop in an area not renowned for them, and found herself to her surprise in a street filled with clothes shops. The rows of shattered windows on either side of the street displayed several ranges of the latest fashions; but she strolled past these looking only for the unimaginative dull blue cotton work clothes which had been the uniform of her youth. Soon she found a shop which stocked what she was looking for. She exchanged one uniform for another, but kept the first with her in her canvas bag in case there was some significance in her being issued with the uniform of the homeland army. Being dressed in the way she wanted to dress, gave her even greater confidence. She left the shop with a decisive step, ready to explore the deserted city and to take on the world.

The street led into a large shopping centre which she did not recognise from previous visits to that area. How much had the streets of the capital changed during the three years she had been away. The goods too had changed, she observed, in development as well as design; but possibly she had simply not noticed them before she left: she had formerly had a complacent attitude of rejection towards progress and the products it created. Now, when those goods no longer filled a want that had been considered a need, she gazed with awe at such ephemera and stopped to look at them in every shop window along the sunny street.

At length the shops gave way to a residential area of trim four-storey terraced houses, their elegant proportions giving them a proud air of grandeur despite their dowdiness from years of neglect. She looked up at the impressive house fronts and remembered when she too had lived in such a house as an impoverished student one hot sunny summer. She had rented a cheap attic bedsitter and used to sunbathe on the roof. One afternoon she had leaned over the parapet and blown soap bubbles down into the street to mystify the passers-by far below. How naïve she had been then, she thought, recalling her eviction for letting a boy sleep in her room overnight. And how naïve the boy had been too, not like the guards in the jails on the other side.

She paused in grief to mourn her lost innocence and the suffering it had involved, her hands resting on a tired fence around a dead garden square. Guilt was a monster like the many-headed hydra; and she had somehow forgotten how to fight it while she was away. She felt certain that sometime before then she had known how to fight guilt and how to win. How else could she have lived with her past?

She walked on more briskly, hastening her steps to escape from that past. Her speed increased rapidly as she was spurred on by her guilt. Soon she was running headlong through the dazzling white streets, fleeing from the hydra she had released from the prison of her mind.

Sheer physical exhaustion forced her to a halt. She drew up some distance away, lungs heaving, heart pounding, legs screaming with the exceptional strain. She bent over to regain her wind and rest her muscles while still on her feet in case she still needed to run. After she had regained her breath, she looked up to see where her flight had brought her.

The street she was in marked the border between the residential area and a neighbouring region of colleges and museums. On the other side of the street a vast ornate building erected in the previous century stood in smoke-stained baroque splendour in a neatly trimmed park. The boundary of the park was lined with mature chestnut trees and tired bushes inside chipped black railings.

So not all the iron railings went in the previous world war, she thought, and added darkly, had they survived another world war too?

A black iron gate swung slowly in the imperceptible breeze, tempting her to leave the glaring city ruins for the restful park which in the dazzling afternoon sun called out to her like an oasis of life in a desert of death. She yielded to the temptation and walked off through the squealing unoiled gate to spend a few minutes among the lush peaceful greens beyond. A goat looked up from grazing the lawns to stare at her in as much surprise as she stared at it. When the goat felt satisfied that she intended it no harm, it gave a dismissive nod of its horned grey head and continued grazing. She strolled past the creature with a benign smile and sat down on a nearby stone bench to watch it as it grazed and wonder how it came to be there.

After a while she became aware of men's voices engaged in conversation. She listened more carefully as the voices came nearer, and looked in their direction but could see no people responsible for the voices, only the goat which continued to graze the lawns. Two unseen men walked up the path to the bench and sat down beside her, the older man on her left side, his younger companion on her right.

'That lecture was a waste of time,' the older man declared.

'The Prime Minister's statement was a load of bull! Take stock of the situation? They're completely ignoring it!' the younger one returned indignantly.

'Surely you have learnt enough by now to ignore any statements from that source,' the older man replied with the condescension of a politician.

'But how much longer will the Government ignore "the possible notion of unseen forces" as you so coyly put it? Why, why, why do we still grovel and scrape to those allies we're supposed to have when they still hold us to financial ransom for their failures?'

'Because greed and deception are the hallmarks of our society, while we still believe in the commercialist dream of spend and waste and profit. Unfortunately the ecologically less extravagant socialists make themselves targets for the ridicule of our self-righteous hypocrites: using force to annex the hinterland for a route to the southern ocean is considered a more serious crime here than using deception to annex the partner's business or the neighbour's wife.'

The voices paused. Still she could see no-one there, not even an astral entity or an etheric ghost to give presence to the voices speaking on her either side. That implied the two men must still be alive, and that what she was hearing was coming from the Akashic Record for that place in response to her desire to know what had happened to the city while she was away.

'Who are you?' she asked.

'But still I didn't think, even in my wildest imagination, that they would totally ignore us!' the young man cried abruptly, ignoring her.

'That is the sort of problem caused by a sweeping electoral victory. The Government is confident that a referendum is not needed..'

'Even though a union ballot is? I piss on this democracy!'

'Stephen...' the older man chided.

The youth gave a perfunctory apology.

'I'm sorry, Dougan. But I've just about had enough.'

'Will you be able to make it to the south coast rally tonight, to work off some of that surplus anger of yours?'

'I'm not sure yet. We're working on a manual of direct action and protest.'

'It's good to be disciplined, Stephen, but it's also good to have some time off. I'll be expecting you at the rally tonight.'

'Acht! The price of peace! All right, Doug: I'll be there.'

Their conversation ended. Their footsteps receded separately from the bench. She gazed along the empty path after them, first in one direction and then in the other; and wondered, as the crumbling buildings wept tears of stone behind her, was this empty city the real price of peace?

CHAPTER 6

As she walked on along the asphalt path, she felt an insistent urge to leave the museum park and rejoin the street. The goat watched her in suspicious silence, still chewing a crop of grass. The exultant birdsong in the bushes suddenly stopped. A new wind blustered through the branches of the chestnut trees. She looked up, recognising the heralds of storm, and discovered that spring had vanished.

Autumn had returned. The trees and bushes were shedding their new leaves in showers of russet and amber. A fierce sunlight scorched the lush green lawns to yellow and parched her burning body. She stripped off her jacket to ease the effects of heat but dared not take off more for fear of being desiccated by that unnatural sun.

She craved water. Her tongue stuck to the roof of her mouth with ravaging thirst. She saw what appeared to be a drinking fountain in an alcove of the shrubs by the railings: a bearded brass gargoyle of pseudo-Classical design; and dragged herself across the dead lawn to try its handle, only to find the fountain did not work. Desperate for water, she pulled the handle again and again but still failed to draw even a drop. At length she stopped, recognising the insidious irrationality of dehydration taking hold. Without water she would soon be dead. She searched on, stumbling out of the sheltered park through the squeaking iron gate and back onto the pale grey pavement beside the glaring white main road.

The wind hit her as soon as she stepped out. Gusts buffeted her body and threw dust in her eyes as though invisible vehicles raced by, fleeing the waterless hole the city had become. She struggled along the pavement, fighting against the unpredictable crosscurrents and tailwinds, clutching at her parched throat, staggering without direction. The merciless elements soon proved too much for her: she collapsed on the pavement, beaten down by the fierce sun. All her thoughts became centred on one thing: water.

In her mind's eye she saw water in rivers, in lakes, in springs, in rain, in puddles, in the sea. She saw all the waters of the earth from afar, and centred her vision on one small plastic cup of water standing there on the paving stone in front of her. She saw herself picking up the cup, sipping the tepid tap water, relishing the metallic taste as it assuaged her thirst. If the locked hotel door had opened for her, she reasoned, could she not also find enough faith to will that cup into being? Voices from the past sang a couplet from a childhood chorus, repeating over and over again in her mind "What, never thirst again? No, never thirst again!" but though she strove to remember the rest of the chorus and find again their faith, the voices would not sing on.

Desperate to save herself, she willed that cup of water to be standing there in front of her and reached out her right hand to grasp it. As her fingers closed on nothing, the plastic cup appeared between them. She picked it up in her shaking hand and gratefully sipped its contents. The tepid water coursed down her parched throat in cooling streams of balm that released her from the merciless punishment of the dry heat. She greedily quaffed the last few mouthfuls and set down the empty cup.

At once her surroundings exploded into life. Along the street an invisible army was marching past the museum. Unseen feet walked over her, trampling her down and kicking her aside. She struggled to stand but was knocked back into the road by the unseen ranks. The men were marching so many abreast that their column seemed to fill the entire width of the thoroughfare. It was impossible to move in any way contrary to their direction: she could only travel with them and try to keep pace with their swift broad strides. Together they marched west into streets of tall rendered brick buildings which contained them like walls. The walls were broken here and there by sheltered alleys which beckoned her to seek refuge in them from the unbending army in the uncompromising streets. Her strides became more diagonal to bring her to the edge of the column. She dived aside out of the ranks of marchers only to be caught up by a different body of invisible people.

The residents of the area were fleeing from the army. Evacuation was destroying the peace of their homes. They protested by running through the side streets back to the areas that had already been cleared. She felt them force her into running with them and tried to keep to the centre of the streets after colliding several times with unseen watchers half-hidden in dark doorways. The crowd led her into a more neglected part of the city, to a region she thought she recognised as a haunt during her years of study at the Academy. In that quarter the students used to live and meet to propound their fiery ideals at gatherings below-ground behind black iron railings in dark dingy basement bars and seedy restaurants whose only claim to culinary distinction lay in the cheap prices of their House Specials.

By chance the mob brought her into the street that Tony's was in, the club she used to frequent. She struggled through the melee, looking out for the old familiar sign, and caught sight of it hanging drunkenly from one chain on an arched iron trellis. Determined to escape the press of the crowd, she flung herself through the archway and down the steps to the basement door and peace. Her head filling with memories, she pushed open the solid black door and walked inside.

Tony's had been her favourite meeting place during her Academy years. It had posed as a club to circumvent licensing laws, but the only entry requirement had been that one knew a person who knew the proprietor's name, Tony Moreno. Many nights she had caroused there with other customers until dawn lit the far side of the sky. At the time she had not noticed how down at heel the club had been; but now in abandonment its seediness was obvious despite the flattering mask of shadows.

She retrieved some candle stubs and matches from a drawer

behind the bar to shed some light on the dismal scene, surprised to find such things still stored there after what must have been far more than three years. Once, candlelight had bathed the tables in a romantic glow. Now it only highlighted the filth on the wooden partitions and the grease-stains on the crumbling white walls. One of the partitions had collapsed, damaging two of the unsteady tables. The white-painted chairs were chipped and yellowing, and covered in dust. The cheerful red and white check tablecloths were grubby grey, the matching café-style curtains were beginning to rot. The floor was littered with broken glass and crockery, all of inferior quality. A more well-equipped and better maintained place would not have fallen so heavily; but still the club's demise brought tears to her eyes.

In that window corner where the curtain now trailed limply, the clown of the class had once forced the club chef to eat his own cooking. Over there on the cabaret square in front of the bar she had danced that erratic tango with the winner of the booby prize in a rag week charity raffle. In that back room they had held endless serious discussions about politics and their individual cure-all solutions to the country's problems.

Now apparently the country had got its cure-all solution; but this was not the answer they had envisioned then. Some might have talked at length of underground publications and amassing guerilla forces and planning hot-blooded civil war; some had even talked of coups d'état; but none had foreseen this eventuality: the broken-hearted capital mourning its departed citizens with tears of stone. No-one had foreseen the fall of Tony's in the storm of change.

She crossed the crockery-strewn floor to see whether the barman's secret cache of house red was still hidden behind the alcove, beneath the dead potted castor oil plants. She found half a case of intact bottles covered in plaster dust and took a bottle back to the bar. From the cupboard of damaged glasses behind the bar she took out a glass with a chipped base and the spare bottle opener which no-one liked using because its handle always cut into the fingers of the hand pulling the cork. She wiped the plaster dust off the glass, the bottle and the bar before opening the wine and setting it out for herself as the barman would have done for her. Then she walked round the bar and sat like a customer on one of the bar stools, to relive those old times.

The cheap red wine still smelt fresh to her when she raised the glass to her lips. Its taste proved palatable though a little flat and metallic with sediment. She could not remember whether that was the wine's natural taste or whether it too had been damaged by the effects of the bombs the city had shared with her. She took another sip and decided that it did not matter much anyway: the cheap red vinegar had always been adequate for her purposes before. Its taste reminded her in particular of a pretentious conversation she had had nine years before with a boyfriend at the far partition table.

'Honey, I've only known you a few days, I know, but I've fallen hopelessly in love with you,' he had said with an insincerity reminiscent of great wits more than half a century before: 'Let's get married and live happily ever after in a garret studio big enough for two.'

'Dearest!' she had returned, with that mocking little laugh she used to affect in her voice, 'We've barely spoken to each other twice. If you feel so desperate for my garret bedsit, let's have an affair. I like to forget things the moment they're done with.'

Affairs had been so fashionable then, especially if one was recovering from a failed one where the ex-partner had been married; but that had only been because they had all been no more than jealous cubs, frightened not only of reality and the responsibilities of emotional entanglement but also of their tawdry stage-managed reputations. Their attitudes had mocked the deep feelings they feared by the enactment of their insincere non-conformism. Nine years later she could see how conformist she had been to their non-conformist society. She had thought herself then to be so liberal and avant garde too; so clever, adaptable, strong, fit, quick-witted, omniscient. Admittedly, she had realised even then she did not have the looks of a television soap queen, but she had made quite an acceptable slightly plainer best friend with all the concomitant virtues of that character's role.

She laughed at herself. The last three years had proved all too conclusively just how naïve, prejudiced, weak, unwise and uninformed she had really been then. Events had cut the world's saviour down to size and proved her to be only another false prophet. Self-opinion's biased mirror had been exchanged for one which could not lie to her, forcing her to see the mewing kitten which ruled the heart of the prowling tiger she had thought herself to be.

She sighed and knocked back her glass of wine. As she brought the glass down again onto the counter her eyes strayed across a radio standing on the work-surface behind the bar. She stepped down off the stool and went behind the bar to try the radio. It proved to be working still though its reception was poor. There was no mistaking the station it was tuned into though, the one station whose broadcast it received: the national radio broadcast by the other side. She froze to hear again those angular accents with the rich tonal cadences, and those tunes the guards had whistled while patrolling the courtyard outside her unreachably high barred fanlight. She raised her empty glass to the radio and cursed the broadcasting country.

Then she noticed the wall-mounted telephone at the end of the bar. It reminded her of her interrupted attempt to phone around from the hotel in search of any remnant of society which might still exist in the country, and sat there offering her a chance to try again. She switched off the radio and lifted the telephone receiver. The dialing tone purred in her ear. Preparing for a long job, she put her jacket back on, brought round her bag and a bar stool, and poured herself a glass of wine. Then she sat down at the telephone and tried to dial out.

She tried the Fairfield number again first, reasoning that if the community was still there as the answering machine suggested, someone should be in the farmhouse preparing the evening meal at that time of day. The call tone gave four rings before it was answered. The line clicked loudly several times and became fuzzy with interference as the woman at the other end began to speak.

'Fairfield Commune,' she announced in a suspicious voice.

'Hello. Is that Shana Daly?' the escaped captive asked. Kaleidoscopic images of the person she had known as Shana Daly filled her thoughts.

'Yes, I am Shana Daly. Why? Who is calling?' the woman demanded with defensive abruptness.

The captive faltered. She could not recall her own name, only the name that others had given her.

'I am called Katy: Katy Brown. You don't know how good it is to hear another voice at last. I finally got back to this country yesterday morning, and I've only heard one person but he's army so he doesn't count. What's happened here?'

In rising panic Shana wanted to put down the phone. Her voice became flustered and uncommunicative.

'I don't know anyone called Katy. You must have got the wrong number....'

'No wait! Don't hang up, please! We used to go to school together, don't you remember? You had to sit in the front row because of the way you mucked around, and I had the desk beside you on your left, which caused us problems 'cause you're left handed and I'm right. Then we left school: you went to uni here in town and I was at the Academy down the road, and we both used to live round the corner from Tony's. And after we graduated you moved north to get out of the rat race, and I followed you up later and got a job thirty miles away from Fairfield working with dogs. Then I disappeared during a touring holiday abroad. Well, now I'm back home. I've managed to escape. I've been out of the country three years going from one prison to another, and I'd really like to know what's happened here while I've been away.'

As Shana listened to her, she felt sick inside. Her sanity was built on insecure foundations which a call like this could easily damage. She dared not tell the caller for she also feared the unknown people who would be listening in to their conversation; but she did want to warn her of her dangerous position, because she too had been a prisoner in her own way, and for a lifetime, not just for three years.

'Look, er, Katy; you clearly know quite a lot about me; but I can't recall you at all. I had no school friends who called themselves Katy. If you are in the capital as you say, you are clearly a stranger in town not to realise how serious your position is; and it's almost curfew so you can't get out tonight. My advice would be to head north tomorrow morning, take a car from someone's garage and as much petrol as you can find – you should still be able to scavenge enough in the suburbs. The roads aren't too good now, but they should be fit enough to get away on if you drive carefully. If you're not stopped, come up here to Fairfield and we'll see what we can do for you. Mind, by the time you arrive here, you won't need much help. Since the war a lot of things have changed.'

'Really? Or do you actually mean you're setting me up, Shana? Your voice has gone all thin, you know, like there's a trap somewhere.'

'I'm afraid that's just what it could turn out to be, Katy. No-one uses phones much these days. The few calls that are made are all monitored.'

A man coughed in the shadows. She spun round to see Smith lounging in the doorway. He looked like a spy from a dated movie with the collar of his light grey raincoat turned up and the brim of his hat turned down at the front. She eyed him with hostility and finished the call.

'You're right, Ma'am: they are monitored. A visitor has just arrived,' she quietly said.

She replaced the receiver and reached down below the bar for another glass to set beside her own, her eyes not leaving Smith for one second. She held up the bottle of wine by the neck for him to see.

'Drink, Smith?' she offered insolently.

He drew a gun from his coat pocket and fired. Green glass and red wine shot across the bar and over her clothes as the bullet shattered the bottle in her hand. Plaster fell from the ceiling with the shock of the report. She dropped the neck of the bottle, thinking that the house red had not been that bad a wine. Her expression was not what Smith wanted to see in her. He walked towards her with an arrogant swagger, the gun in his hand levelled at her heart.

'I arrest you for looting goods from two shops this afternoon and for lighting this room without covering the windows after curfew in a blackout zone. If you resist arrest you will be shot,' he spat.

'Oh. So you're a policeman,' she said.

He could see none of the fear in her which he was trying to invoke. Indeed, she rather seemed relieved to face again the old routine of threat and violence; as though the bullet through her heart would be an acceptable method of escape, because afterwards there would be no possibility of recapture, and because the responsibility would be his for murder, not hers for suicide.

'All citizens can act as police and have some powers of arrest,' he said.

He pointed his gun to the ceiling in a big gesture to demonstrate that he was uncocking the trigger. She watched with contempt and defiantly threw his threat back at him.

'Then I arrest you, Smith, for kidnapping me and for stealing some of my personal possessions while I was your prisoner, asleep in the hotel room where you kept me.'

Her defiance told him she had endured so much in the last three years that she had gone beyond the captive's toneless defeatism: she actively courted death to save herself even more suffering.

'You have started a very foolish game, Katy,' he warned: 'I could have arrested you for failing to produce your identity papers on demand, and for that you would be shot.'

'And you would do that if necessary, would you, Smith? You would shoot me for failing to have what you stole from me? For my papers were in my possession when you exchanged me for the documents on the bridge. Ask the Allied guards.'

Smith slipped the gun back into his pocket and sat down on the bar stool to reason with her.

'Look, Katy, wouldn't it be better if we were both a bit more civilised about this? I don't want to hurt you. I would rather be your friend.'

'So you can have a clearer conscience about getting me to betray myself? There is nothing to betray. I went on holiday; I got arrested, I was imprisoned, I was exchanged, I was exchanged, end of story; now can I go home?'

'Not yet. We need to know how you were treated. We have to know what you said.'

'So I am still not free!' she cried, crashing her fist down on the counter.

She grasped the legs supporting the counter in manic rage and with a mighty heave overturned the bar onto Smith. He stepped back off the stool before the counter caught his legs, but missed his footing on some shards of glass and fell to the floor. Before he had a chance to recover she had leapt over the upturned counter, grabbed her bag and fled through the door.

She sprinted up the steps to the street, hoping to see Smith's small black car parked at the kerb, but the road was empty. Instead, she darted down an alley into the maze of back streets behind Tony's, hoping to lose Smith quickly in the maze so that she could go on to find some shelter for the night before the curfew enforcers came out on patrol. She managed to lose herself in the maze too.

Some time later she came out onto a more familiar road again, down by the river. To her right lay an industrial belt, to her left a modern residential area. She looked up at the tall apartment buildings remembering the terraces which had stood there before, and marvelled yet again at a borough administration which had continued to spend money on such urban constructions long after their social disadvantages had been discovered and their design recognised to be faulty.

That administration had long since gone. She too could go the same way, depending on the decisions she made as she coped with the strange conflicting dangers in the post-war city. She was hungry, and her body had few reserves to live on after the punishing prison regime. She also felt exhausted after living a day of recurring shocks as she confronted all the changes in the capital. Food and shelter had to be her priorities at that point.

She caught sight of a looted corner shop at a junction with a side street and headed towards it hoping that she might find some tinned food there. As she crossed the road towards it she suddenly felt very unprotected and quickened her pace. A few moments later she heard the distant roar of a diesel engine. She dived through the smashed door into the shop and hid behind the ransacked window display cabinet.

An army transporter roared past with blazing headlights and flapping canvas sides, its main beams flooding the shop and dazzling her eyes. Alarmed that she might have been spotted, she stayed hidden behind the cabinet for some time after the lorry had passed before she felt confident enough to come out again.

The shop had been one of those general stores which stock almost every basic one might require for everyday living. The food shelves had long since been stripped bare, but when she searched more methodically by the light of a candle stub she had pocketed at Tony's she did find a few battered tins below the shelves in a corner of the floor. She threw the tins into her bag, together with a small sharp piece of metal to use as an improvised tin opener, and hurried back out into the dark street.

The looted shop and the nearby buildings would seem obvious lairs, she realised, reviewing her position from Smith's point of view. To stay one step ahead of him she moved on and walked some distance before she began to look for a place to shelter for the night. She holed up in one of the deserted riverside factories to the southwest of the shop, camping in one of the offices for the night. After dining at a large managerial desk on cold tinned macaroni cheese and new potatoes, she made a bed from two soft office chairs and lulled herself to sleep planning what to do the next day.

CHAPTER 7

The new day dawned with that brilliance in the spring sun which heralds summer warmth. Bright sunny beams shafted through the grimy office window and woke the escaped captive lying there on her couch of office chairs. She yawned sleepily and stretched her sluggish body. As her mind cleared, she realised that for once she welcomed the new day. Though the old resentments were there as always, threatening to dominate her mood for the day should she not evict them from her mind; still she woke with the awareness that this day held promise for her, more promise than any other day had held in the last three years. It even surpassed the day of her release two days before, for that promise had been based on false hopes. She should have remembered that in the end all the sides always proved to be the same.

She breakfasted on tinned apricots and custard, which satisfied her thirst as well as her hunger, and dutifully filed all the empty tins in a convenient rubbish bin. Then she left the office to explore the factory.

First she looked for a washroom and found one on the same floor. To her delight the sink taps still turned to give running water, albeit of a muddy brown colour. She stripped off the clothes she was wearing and soaked them to dislodge the red wine stains while she washed herself down and dressed in her army khaki.

As she was moving her personal effects from blue cotton pockets to khaki wool ones, she discovered that she was carrying some identification papers after all, in her bag. She paused to read through them to find out who her homeland thought she was.

The papers stated that she was thirty-one year-old Katherine

Brown, a photographer from the midlands whose present address was care of her guardian and employer Mr John Smith of Smith and Son Ltd. for whom she worked as a photographic reporter with *Now!* Magazine. All at once several things moved into place in her mind; but not about Smith, rather about her own past.

Though she still did not know precisely who she was, and she still did not know who had made the mistake in her identity; at least she now understood who everyone else thought her to have been through the last three years, a mistake which had cost her dearly. Now she understood why Shana Daly had not recognised her during their telephone conversation. And now she knew which direction to take that day, for though she did not yet know who she was, she could still remember the southern suburb where her parents lived. She could even picture their large detached house, and hoped it was still in as good condition as the factory around her, for that would mean there was a remote chance that her parents were still alive despite everything that had happened.

With freshened body and more confident mind she continued to explore the factory. She was hoping to find some clues in the documents or the building which would give her a better idea of what had happened in the capital. As she searched she kept remembering Shana's comment that since the war a lot of things had changed; but the way the factory had been left did not seem to bear that comment out. Except for the dusty piles of clothes lying everywhere the place looked more as though the workers had taken a tea break rather than been disturbed by the outbreak of war. She walked down a production line of toy dolls and noticed how a pile of clothes was lying at each workstation. With an increasingly sickened feeling in the pit of her stomach she gradually realised that those dusty clothes were all that remained of the people who had worked there assembling those dolls, that each little pile was a dead body.

She turned away in horror and dashed across the production

floor to escape the nightmare world she had stumbled into by chance. In the empty corridor she felt a little easier: at least the dust on that lino-covered empty floor was not the remains of some human being but a natural accumulation after years of neglect. She pushed through the heavy swing doors at the end of the corridor onto the landing and noticed that the dust on the stairs had recently been disturbed. The quartzes glinted in the pink stone steps more brightly within the outlines of what looked like descending footprints too large to be her own. Despite her better judgement she chose to follow. The footprints led her to a side entrance on the ground floor and outside into the loading bay. There the footsteps vanished. Looking right, she could see a low wall at the front of the factory. She walked out onto the street.

The factory service road ran parallel with the river on its north bank. Her parents' home lay some twelve or fourteen miles south of the river. She turned right and headed in a westerly direction hoping the street would bring her out onto the main road to the nearest bridge. Her pace was brisk at first, and because the area seemed deserted again she sang folk songs to keep herself in step.

Suddenly a man appeared ahead of her, khaki clad; strolling out of a factory entrance and turning left towards her. Her heart pounding in alarm, she kept to her strict pace to maintain an air of confidence, glad that she was wearing the khaki uniform again because it might make him assume she had a legitimate purpose in being there. As they closed, she noticed his rank insignia of an army captain. She had no indication of rank or even regiment on her uniform. Would he arrest her or denounce her, she wondered, or would she be able to bluff him about her presence in the area.

'Good morning, civilian,' he greeted firmly in a well-educated accent..

'Good morning, Captain,' she replied, clearly intending to walk past him.

He fell in step beside her on her left side, between her and the road, easily matching her pace. She stopped and looked up into his face. He was a tall tired man with a preoccupied air. His spirit within was in a darkness unlike her own, for his soul was no golden helix spinning in space but a small boy drowning in mire. She flashed a not quite welcoming smile at him and walked on at a more leisurely pace.

'I hadn't realised that they are permitting civilians back into this quadrant,' he said.

She stalled for time, weighing up the possible implications of his comment. Though it sounded only as though he was making conversation he could be starting a veiled interrogation.

'Hadn't you? They haven't, really. I'm a sort of special case,' she said.

'One of the census chaps, you mean, here to find out who's dead?' he asked, gesturing to the surrounding factories.

His strained manner betrayed his preoccupation with matters other than the official purpose for his presence there. Though his duty might be reconnaissance or patrol, his thoughts churned in the turmoil of emotional shell-shock. She thought carefully before she replied, knowing a person who was that distracted could react with dangerous unpredictability.

'No: rather looking for signs of life. And you?'

'Same as you, following up the report of the looter seen in this area last night. No stolen goods in your bag, I hope,' he joked.

'Of course not!' she laughed, but hastily tried to change subject before the sum of clues gave him the right answer. 'It's heartrending, this; what's happened to our lovely city.'

'It could have been worse: we were all expecting H bombs or A bombs, not N bombs. Destroys the people without destroying the property. Good capitalistic attitude, eh? Shame it was the commies who dropped them.'

'Ah, but what did we do back, Captain? If there's one thing this war has taught me, it's that no matter what side we may be on, we're all the same in the end.'

He stopped her abruptly.

'That's traitorous talk, civilian! Show me your papers!'

His rebuke and the grip of his right hand on her left arm made her flinch. She realised that he had been trying to draw her with his comments about bombs: he had not been expressing a personal view. She obediently handed over her identity papers. He looked through the documents so hastily he fumbled over some of the pages. When he saw her profession and her employment, he nodded with a knowing exclamation. His demeanour changed to a sneer as he handed the papers back to her.

'A member of the propaganda machine, I see, Miss Brown: write one thing and think another.'

Such a blatant expression of bitterness surprised her. She felt a pang of compassion for him which was not quite masked by her own bitterness after her recent experiences.

'You're sick, Captain,' she warned in a low forceful voice to demoralise him and so prevent him from questioning her further: 'I can feel it, I can see it, I can hear it. Your mind's so torn apart you're not fit for duty.'

Her attack moved the verbal skirmish to his own territory. He recoiled defensively with that cynical hopelessness which had become such a prevalent attitude in the armed forces.

'Maybe, Katherine Brown; but what would happen to me if I was discharged? And what would happen to the country if all the rest of us were discharged? Have you told your readers that?'

She looked searchingly into his face for a moment until she saw that his bitterness was general rather than personally directed at her. She broke her gaze from him to put her papers away. When he said nothing further, she looked back to read his expression again.

'Are you really what the army's become?' she asked, the pity in her voice mixed with contempt. 'Good day, Captain. I have got work to do.'

She gave him a curt nod and marched off along the road. He did not follow.

CHAPTER 8

She was on familiar ground at last, walking south along the commonside road towards the suburb where she had been schooled. The area had then been the sort of place the residents had still called a village. Now the residents had gone, taking their whimsical fancies with them. The fast main road traffic had gone too: for once she could enjoy the walk along the edge of the bedraggled common. Though the bushes and trees looked cleaner to her, they were still unhealthy. They had endured a long primary poisoning from the traffic before the secondary poisoning during the war. On her left she walked past high brick walls and secretive drives leading to impressive detached houses. She had often dreamed as a child of owning such a house herself one day, but in adulthood had made that ambition dependent upon her commercial success as an artist, only to find herself too unworldly and idealistic to achieve such success.

The dishonesty of that excuse suddenly became apparent to her. She laughed out loud at herself for the false pride which still tainted her thoughts despite all the events of the last three years. The honest explanation for her lack of success was a combination of her mediocre talent, her poor application and her failure to move with the times. Instead of allowing commercial pressures and social influences to mould her creativity and inspire her to new work, she had hidden herself away in the countryside near that minor northern city and supported herself as a kennel maid so that she could paint canvasses of demons at a time when society refused to acknowledge the power of evil and poured scorn on any belief in the Evil One. She had been a failure as an artist because she preferred to stay in her familiar old rut rather than face a new challenge.

She laughed at herself more gently. That did not make her

guilty of anything. Then why did such a self-assessment make her blush with shame? In the circumstances it mattered little whether she was a conservative or an adventurous artist, for either way she would still have been caught up in the war and in this chilling aftermath where art had little value compared with resourcefulness. Had she been commercially successful or critically acclaimed she would have found the fall of her homeland a far more devastating blow to her lifestyle and her ambitions than she was finding it as a failed artist who had a way with animals.

At least she was alive: the owners of those luxurious houses were not. Now she could simply break in to take possession of one should she so desire. She chose not to because she would rather acquire ownership legally. Her imagination played on the possibilities of their vacant possession: perhaps when the country was sufficiently stable, land would be portioned out among the survivors and she would be able to claim one of the houses there for herself. And she would keep a string of horses and go riding on the common along the gravel and shingle paths she had ridden as a child.

The village looked unchanged, as though she had happened to be walking through it early on some Sunday morning. There were few signs of the pillagers there, either along the High Street or in the apartment buildings on the hill.

Halfway down the hill stood the school she had attended as a senior. Originally two houses, it was a much extended establishment, more ugly than she had remembered it because of the addition of a new science block. Already the new extension looked less sound than the buildings it linked. She walked past the long frontage and peered down the side lane past the kitchens where the grey squirrels used to wait for scraps. No grey squirrels waited there now. She set foot inside the gate. At once her inner sense warned her she should leave. Ignoring the foreboding, she walked on to the porch and the main entrance.

She had always remembered the school to be an attractive

building inside, full of dark woods and white walls. When she pushed open the entrance door, a faint smell of polish and paper also came back; that distinctive smell of that particular school which until then she had forgotten. She had also forgotten how tempting that staircase past the front door had been to run down, with its sharp twist and the stout handrail the students had swung on when they descended in a hurry to the basement rooms. She could almost feel some girls rush past her as she ascended with a more mature step to the landing above. To her right opened the doors to the secretary's office and the head's study. Ahead stood the double swing doors to the school hall.

She hesitated before entering the hall, her hand on the door panel, uncertain of what she would find on the far side. She had always remembered the hall with fondness: its balcony and its pleasing proportions, its polished wood floor and its battered creaking stage with the grand piano at the back and the lectern in the middle; and the old prints on the walls between the classroom doors. Gathering what courage she could, she pushed through the swing doors and walked into a scene of horror.

In neat rows on the polished floor lay more than three hundred little piles of winter uniforms: blue skirts and jumpers, sensible shoes and white shirts, and the old school ties. Hymn 293 they had sung that fateful morning assembly, but no valour could have saved them from their tortured death that day. She heard their screams filling her mind's ear and screamed with them as she turned about and fled.

She fetched up against the red brick wall outside the school to weep for all the young lives that had been lost there so needlessly. The flower of the capital's southern suburbs had fallen there; a generation of young women prevented by fate from fulfilling their true potential. She, and her friend Shana, were probably the only ones left still living who had attended that school, she realised. The thought placed a cloak of responsibility upon her shoulders to make her life reflect that privilege and to prove that though the girls had died with no chance to save themselves, at least they had not died in vain.

Through the veil of tears her eyes happened to gaze upon the church next door to the school. The church seemed to beckon her inside to grieve in a more appropriate place, as though it was indecent for her to mourn in the street. She walked slowly along the pavement, remembering previous visits to the church when the school had marked the Christian festivals; of crocodiles of winter-hatted girls laughing and joking with one another as they tried not to walk on the cracks between the grey paving slabs, and the form mistress's baleful glare to remind them they were misbehaving in public. Then, the heavy church doors had been open; but now they were shut. She placed her right palm by the edge of the right-hand door and gently put pressure on the wooden panel. The door swung silently inwards. She pushed it further open and walked inside, letting the outer door slowly shut of its own accord behind her.

At first the church seemed to be in darkness. She turned to pull the outer door back open but found her feet held by the heavy coir doormat. Her eyes gradually adjusted to the gloom and she began so see a dim glow coming though the half-glazed inner doors. She passed on through the second doorway into the dim interior of the church. With those few steps she felt as though she was walking out of the world's conflicts into a realm of peace and mediaeval sanctuary. With the unthinking habit of custom she briefly bowed her head to the altar and walked on down the aisle.

As a child she had not looked at this church at all: it had simply been a large dark place she had visited occasionally and had always seen from a pew behind a pillar. With adult eyes and understanding she could see that the interior of the building was far more attractive than she had appreciated as a child; a lot smaller too, and clearly still well cared for. She sat down on the front pew in the closest congregational seat to the altar rail and contemplated the traditional design and decoration of the sanctuary.

No cross stood on the naked altar: no symbol of the building's purpose remained beyond the lofty chancel arch. She cried out in dismay. Her sanctuary was a false one. Robbed of its traditional status, the church could afford her no protection other than that offered by its walls and roof. She had been wrong to consider herself safe there from Smith, and from the Captain and the army he represented. With her disappointment showing clearly in her face she stood up to leave.

'Wait, my child,' said a man's voice.

He had spoken softly from the shadows of the north side pews where somehow she had always sat as a child. She turned her head slightly in his direction, unsure of what she would see. He kept hidden in the shadows, concerned not to frighten her in any way.

'Who are you?' she asked.

'I am the Minister of this church. For two years I have been waiting for a congregation, since the last of the survivors left. Are you among the first to be allowed back?'

'But this is no longer a church. There is no cross on the altar.'

He identified the defensive way she avoided answering his question to be an indication of her fear and sought to reassure her.

'The church is not the building or the altar or the cross; but the body of believers with Christ at its head. Are you a believer?'

'No!' she shouted, driven by an inner compunction which overrode her thoughts yet was not of her.

'Then why are you here?' he asked gently.

She leapt up in blustering indignation.

'I'm quite happy to go!"

'That was not what I meant, child,' he reassured. 'This city is large, and there are many buildings in it, but very few indeed still with a human presence; perhaps only this one. So what did bring you to this church?'

She ignored his question, defensive still.

'Why don't you come out and show yourself, Minister?' she demanded.

He waited a moment before quietly answering her.

'I do not wish to alarm you. I do not look quite how I used to look. I was in the basement working on the boiler when the blast happened down the road. The boiler shielded half of me from the withering wind, the rest of me not quite so well.'

She nodded and sat down again, her manner cynical and rebellious against events.

'Take confidence, Minister, and step out of the shadows into the light. I have also been scarred, but my scars are all in my mind. I have been a prisoner for more than two years. They are all the same, scars. Your looks are deformed, my thoughts are deformed.'

She paused, as chaotic images raced through her mind, raising a tempest of emotions. To her own surprise words poured out of her that she could barely comprehend.

'There is a demon in my mind that bends my conscious thoughts and places me in conflict with myself, so that I cannot speak the truth at certain times because it prevents me from remembering the truth I used to believe. For we are both speaking inside me, and I am compelled to listen; but I have two masters to obey, and they are incompatible. The stronger one directed me, but the weaker one defends its stronghold in my... It orders me to deny... It will not let me say.'

She broke down and wept with the stresses of the conflict in her mind. His heart went out to her in compassion. He prayed to God for divine inspiration to give him the right words and for healing to make the troubled young woman whole again. He also felt gratitude, for though time was running out for him, he still had a divine purpose, to care for this new member of his congregation after two years of caring for naught but bricks and mortar in the service of the Architect of the Universe.

He stepped out of the shadows and his doubts to offer her

his whole right hand, and felt as though he moved beyond mere physical light into divine effulgence. He could do little for his own condition, perhaps, but that did not lessen his ability to invoke God's blessing on this sick child or to be the channel through which such a blessing could flow. Indeed, he sensed that this healing was the purpose behind his own reprieve. Eighteen months, the emergency medical team had given him, but the life expectancy of a person with his degree of neutron bomb frostbite had usually proved to be far less. And there had been a great many of them who had been touched by that withering wind. Most of the millions or more treated with him in the capital's hospitals afterwards had then left the city; but he with his injuries and his vocation had been permitted to stay. It had been a lonely existence in such a vast hermitage, until this frightened young woman had walked in.

He approached her with care so that she would see his whole right side first rather than his blackened and wasted left side. He ran his fingers through his straight silvery-grey hair to make it cover more of the dying left side of his face and so prevent his deformities from frightening her too much.

'Take comfort, my child,' he reassured: 'You are welcome to stay here for as long as you wish; and while you are here you are not obliged to leave the city, for though there is no cross on the altar, that is only because both the brass cross and the wooden cross were stolen during the evacuation. This church is still sanctified and can be a sanctuary to you.'

'Thank you, Minister.'

She slowly turned her head to look at him. Prepared by his words to expect to see severe deformity, the first indications did not revulse her. He relaxed a little and turned his body to face her more. As she began to appreciate the full extent of his injuries, she felt great pity for him, mingled with gratitude that her own circumstances had not given her such cause for sorrow. In comparison with his suffering, her trials as a captive were negligible, mere privations from which she could recover should she develop the right attitudes to life. He could not recover, and his loss would be all the harder for him to bear because he knew what it had felt like to be whole. For him, his consolation lay in his belief that through his undeserved injuries he was sharing in the sufferings of Christ.

'I'm sorry, Father. I should be offering my help to you,' she said.

He smiled reflectively and sat down near her on the neighbouring pew, still keeping his better side towards her.

'It's a long time since I've heard someone express a thoughtful sentiment like that. This nation became very selfish because of this war.'

'What happened?' she asked.

He looked at her inquiring expression and realised that she genuinely did not know, that her imprisonment had somehow prevented her from hearing any news. Her question gave him a legitimate reason to let his thoughts go back. Recently he had not allowed himself that luxury because of the bitterness evoked by his memories of the war.

'April the sixth, the year before last,' he began: 'It was a fresh spring day, shortly before Easter. The garden was filled with birdsong – it woke us up. At breakfast I decided I ought to take a look at the church boiler as it had made some odd noises during the last service. Martha chose to go shopping, to lay up stocks for Holy Week – always an especially busy time for us. She was pleased to be able to get down to the supermarket before the rush. Have you seen the supermarket now?'

She shook her head. 'No, but I can picture what it's like,' she said.

'At fourteen minutes past nine the first bomb struck. Others followed in quick succession, all over the capital, all over the country; wiping out all the cities, destroying all the centres of population. The nearest one landed down the road, about three miles away on top of the underground terminus - close enough to kill; far enough away for it not to be quite instant. I was told the blasts somehow burst cell walls, by sort of boiling off the water inside. People close by died instantly of massive desiccation; those further away around here, rather more slowly; and of course, I was protected by several layers of stone and a boiler: I was only hit by a weak reflection of its full blast. That is why I survived as well as I did. Very few survivors from this area. Because it was such a lovely spring day.'

He lapsed into thought, walking back through his memories on his own. She sensed he needed prompting to continue and tried by describing some of her own experiences.

'I saw the children in the school next door, the rows and rows of uniforms in the hall. I didn't appreciate the full horror of it all until then. I used to go into that hall for assembly too, just as they had gone. Did it come as complete a surprise as it looked?'

'Yes,' he said. 'There was no four minute warning. We had been misinformed – there was no warning at all. Perhaps it was better that way. I can still remember that morning's paper, the front-page headlines about progress in the arms talks, and I praised the Lord that common sense was prevailing about atomic weapons at last. But that had been my mistake. If you read the article, you will find that only H bombs and A bombs were mentioned.'

'And what hit the country were N bombs?'

He nodded. 'They destroy the populace without destroying the property, a bit like fumigation; and we all perished just like vermin in our holes and on our runs through that deadly withering wind.'

She nodded, wondering how that descriptive phrase about the neutron bombs had circulated enough to be used by both Ministers and army Captains, when communications media appeared to be non-existent.

'I regained consciousness some time later,' he continued: 'I was in a lot of pain. I remember thinking, the birds aren't singing any more – they must have been frightened by the bang.

Then I hauled myself outside and saw what had really happened to them.'

He paused a moment to mourn the birds, and then continued, 'I quickly barricaded myself in at home for protection, thinking I was going to get radiation sickness. We didn't know, you see. None of us expected this. We thought it would be all or nothing, not this halfway in between. I turned on the radio. Did you know that most of the Continent has gone? All I picked up was one of those pirate stations out at sea. Terrified, those young men were. Martha was dead, of course. I found her remains in the supermarket. Naturally I buried her. I spent a lot of the first year burying people. But then I realised the scale of the thing, that I could spend the rest of my life burying people. So then I simply laid the city to rest. I left your school as a memorial. I left all the rest as memorials too, and I came back here to die.'

He looked up at her and smiled gently. 'But God had other plans. I think you are part of that plan. So tell me, child, what happened to you?'

She breathed in ready to answer but hesitated and suddenly broke down in tears. In the feeble frame of that dying man she had found the spiritual pillar her soul had yearned for during the past two years. His sympathy cut through the wall of inhibitions she had laboriously built up to protect herself, and so released all the pent-up emotions dammed behind. He cradled her head on his good shoulder as her body shook with the violence of her sobs, and spoke words of reassurance to calm her. In time her grief subsided and she began to find the words to tell him what had happened to her.

She started with the holiday: the preparations she and her nine friends and acquaintances had made, their excitement as they left, and the fun they had had touring through the countries to the west of the other side; countries which, he informed her, had all suffered the fate of their own. She told him about the unexplained gap in her memory, the missing months which had taken her from a hotel to a prison. She described her treatment at the hands of her captors, and how that treatment had proved to be the same at both ends of the political spectrum and on either side of the fence. And she showed him the papers she found in her bag that morning which she presumed had been given her by Smith during their violent meeting at Tony's.

'But I am not Katherine Brown the photographer, and she would never have let herself be called Katy. Kathy, perhaps, Kath mostly; but never Katy. I know: she was one of the organisers of the trip. We did look quite similar then, I admit; but we were not alike. She was much more successful with the camera than I was with acrylics and pastels, at least from the looks of her clothes. Yet she's the person all the sides think I am, and that is how they have all treated me.'

'But if you are not her, then who are you?' he asked.

She hesitated. The pause drew his attention. A subtle change came over her manner and a flat confident tone altered her voice.

'I am Kath Brown the photographer,' she said.

He nodded thoughtfully, sensing he had seen this so-called demon of hers before in others. He asked another question to test whether the phenomenon was psychological rather than spiritual.

'What were you doing in the eastern countries, beyond just taking a holiday?'

Again she hesitated: the subtle difference changed her manner, the flat confidence altered the way she spoke.

'I was photographing defence installations so that the allied military authorities could reconstruct the lay-outs and work out the purpose of the bases.'

Her answer sounded as if she had read it from a script, it was so long and involved.

'But you just told me you were an artist. You're not a photographer at all,' he said.

'All photographers are artists. Photography is a form of art as well as a method of documentation.'

'Of course, Kath: I should have realised. But there was an artist on the bus with you, wasn't there, a girl who looked quite like you. What was her name?'

'I am Kath Brown, the photographer.'

He gave up his questions and hugged her to his shoulder in compassion. Her escape from the devastation of the bombs had occurred because she had fallen victim to a different kind of political destruction, a mental reprogramming that had superimposed several false memories in her mind, probably through the use of violence and drugs rather than hypnosis. Even these psychological demons could be exorcised by the power of God, creator of the human mind and of the entire universe in which microscopic humanity existed.

He prayed silently for divine guidance, and became aware that to undo the work others had wrought in her, he needed to dissociate her attention from her senses so that the automatic commands in her subconscious could be erased while she was off guard. He lit two candles and placed them on the altar where their small flickering lights would claim her attention. The candles were reflected in the polished stonework of the sanctuary, creating a visual aura of holiness and peace.

She gazed on the trembling flames, recalling the candles in Tony's. The holiness of the sanctuary seemed to be out of reach because of all that she had done wrong. Kaleidoscopic scenes from her memory took her further back into her past, to a time when she used to worship and thought nothing of reciting the general confession. Now, those words were inordinately difficult to say. In a trembling voice she whispered, 'Forgive me, Father, for I have sinned.'

He sat back down beside her.

'Yes, child?'

Tears returned to her eyes. She began to speak, of all the bitterness and hatred, the selfishness and enmity she had felt during the last two years. He listened in silence, letting her release the tide of negativity, noting that she was trying not to lay blame on anyone but herself. Her confession continued with her memories from further back in her past. Clearer and clearer became the details as she recalled her life before the touring holiday: her frustrations and loneliness but for her beloved dogs and her painting; her ingratitude for all the good things she had been given in that earlier life; the times she had wanted to die.

When her words ran out they sat in silence for some time. Then he absolved her with words from chapter seven of the book of Micah:

'Lord, *who is a God like you, pardoning iniquity, and passing over the transgression of the remnant of your possession? He does not retain his anger for ever, because he delights in showing clemency. He will again have compassion upon us; he will tread our iniquities under foot. You will cast all our sins into the depths of the sea.'*

The words seemed to make an arch around her. A sense of peace flooded her whole being. The heavy grimy coat of her past sloughed off her shoulders, leaving her radiant and free. The golden helix was spinning so fast that she could not make out its design. Beyond it, the cottage of her psyche was gleaming in sunlight. She walked up the path through the cottage garden of delphiniums and hollyhocks, to the radiantly yellow front door. The door opened, and she could see through the hallway into the rooms on her right and on her left. But across the room in front of her stood a black wall, a cube she could not penetrate. Wordlessly she prayed for the whole of the cottage to be open to God, for the black cube to be removed. She concluded the prayer by thanking God, knowing that her petition would be answered soon and the black cube would somehow go.

The Minister set out bread and wine on the altar, and recited the passage from 1 Corinthians 11 recalling the institution of the Lord's Supper, the memorial of Jesus' last meal with his disciples before his death. She watched, aware of a distracting conflict in her subconscious, telling her to leave at once. She directed the peace she was also feeling to dampen the strident voices of rebellion. The Minister began to recite the Lord's Prayer. Her lips moved silently recalling the words with him. He offered her the sanctified bread and wine softly intoning the words of distribution. She shared the symbolic meal with him in silence. The soda bread was rough and coarse; the wine had the intense flavour of a sherry. The physical nature of the elements of the meal did not detract from their power to heal.

She saw again the open door of that cottage, the black cube in front of her in the hall. Cautiously she raised her right hand and placed her palm against the black wall. Through the touch she was pulled through the dark infinity of space towards what looked at first like sunlight. The light evolved into the purer and infinitely more powerful blue-white blaze of glory and love which she had seen once before: God's light, in which the golden helix of her soul spun joyously, radiating white light itself from the spark of God at its core. For a few moments she relaxed there in the healing warmth of divine effulgence.

Slowly the bright light faded as temporal concerns drew her back into the material world. Her mind ached briefly, a passing symptom from the process of being made whole again. The psychological controls in her psyche had been broken by the power of God's love. She had been released from bondage. The captive was free.

'I am Sarah Baylis,' she said.

She paused to wonder at the miracle of knowing her true identity again after two years of unknowing. At length she continued.

'No wonder Shana Daly didn't remember me. I must go....'

The Minister caught her left hand as she rose to her feet.

'No, wait,' he appealed.

She looked at him and remembered the part he had played in her release. With a grateful apology she sat down again, and stayed.

Part 2

…. And Beyond

CHAPTER 9

Three days later Sarah set out again, in a small red car the Minister had given her. She had laid him to rest the evening before, after his body gave up the unequal fight to stay alive. Their time together had transformed her.

He had helped her come to terms with her experiences enough to be forgiving rather than resentful towards those who had wronged her. He had also helped her interpret the visions she had experienced on her return to the homeland, as coming from her innate ability to discern through the spiritual gift of Knowledge, skewed by the as yet unclear events of those missing few months, and further distorted by a psychoactive substance in the cigarettes Smith had given her.

No longer did she need other people to give her identity purpose now. She had gained confidence through re-identifying herself with her baptismal name Sarah, but sensed that it was important for her to continue using the identity of Katherine Brown for the moment while her situation was still unclear. As memories of some of her lost experiences returned, she began to understand that she had somehow been used as an innocent political pawn, though how and to what end was still a mystery. She set out, resolving to solve that mystery so that she could legitimately re-assume her real identity and become truly free.

She drove on into the freshness of a new spring day. All around her from the stone and concrete of the city suburbs a new song was being sung, a faint echo from the gardens and the parks of a mightier song of renewal being sung by the rivers hidden beneath the roads and the countryside beyond the city limits. The earth was healing itself at last. A summer of death had passed, followed by a summer of decay; and now at last was dawning a summer of rebirth. Not all the birds had died. A few had already ventured back into the cement and asphalt desert, bringing more. Soon the land would rise up from the grave.

Then she remembered Smith. Her buoyant mood vanished. Smith was not the sort of man to go away while she had hidden in the sanctuary of the church. He would have used the time to track her down and catch up with her; and then wait unseen in shelter until she made her next move. She wondered what it was he wanted to know. Perhaps he thought that she was Kath Brown and expected her to lead him to her fellow conspirators. Or perhaps he knew that she was not and followed her until she unearthed the proof he needed to discredit others. Certainly he did not follow her purely for herself. What had those others done or had done to them for him to be so interested in her? And why had she survived when so many others had not?

Three miles down the road her car entered the region bordering the epicentre of the nearest bomb blast. She turned right at a roundabout to drive to the underground terminus but found the street blocked with rubble and debris from the explosion. An insistent call she would rather have ignored compelled her to park the car and walk through the street and her fears to see for herself what man had done to man.

The bomb had landed on the bus terminal outside the underground station, demolishing the tiled station parade, the road bridge over the shunting tracks, the curved office block nearby and the cinema opposite. On the other side of the street the front of the shopping parade had been torn off. The broad road between was impassible with rubble. A lone traffic light poked blindly out of the debris, near some mangled red aluminium which was the remains of a bus. There was no sign of burning: all the destruction appeared to have been caused by the impact and the detonation of the force the bomb had contained.

Not quite the perfect bomb, she thought cynically, for in action it had destroyed property as well as people. Her moral outrage countered that compared with the near annihilation of the local populace, the destruction of property was negligible.

Yet there were no bodies there, for all the thousands killed by that one blast. There were no little piles of clothes among the rubble on the masonry-strewn pavements. Two years had passed since this unremarkable suburban centre had become the epicentre of that bomb: the destruction of the blast and the erosion of two seasonal cycles had dispersed even the smallest scrap of human form.

She stopped and swore, turning round on herself in mental anguish as she relived the murders of those faceless people whose blood still cried out from the bricks and mortar. School friends had come from this suburb; their parents and kin had lived and worked here. Those people were not faceless, nor were their voices unknown. They existed in her past and they had died here too: Pradesh and Marion and Christina and Eric and Peter and Shaheen and Niamh and Harry and a hundred others whose lives had touched her own. What had they done wrong that had earned them this death penalty? They had not joined the forces; so why had they been fated to die by that bomb without even a warning that they should prepare themselves to die?

The deaths of unknown nameless faceless people were just casualties of war; but the death of a friend or relative or childhood companion was murder; and the deaths of so many known named people whose faces she could recall in a multitude of moods, that was massacre, mass murder. The people who had occasioned these deaths were murderers who deserved the penalty for mass murder; and the people who had stored up the weapons capable of such massacre, did so with intent to commit murder, whatever mitigating circumstances they might plead; with cold-blooded intent to break the sixth commandment.

Were none innocent of this bloodshed, she asked herself. Her judgement of this crime against humanity indicted her own country too, and through it even herself, the one who was passing such judgement. Her homeland too had stockpiled those weapons and had invested a significant proportion of its revenue in a terrifying arsenal of death; and it too had stored up as a deterrent enough nuclear weapons to make its leaders capable of destroying the whole world in their claimed desire to enable the country to protect itself. It had also invited its supposed allies to place their weapons of war upon its soil; and the allies were such warmongers that they had pressed for the invitation in their negotiations by blackmailing her homeland with its national debt. So her country had said yes to an intention to commit mass murder, despite the protests of a significant proportion of its people, and yet it had still claimed it was a Christian democracy. When had the vote been taken by the people in a referendum on that issue alone? Yet here they had died for what they had not chosen. And she was no mere innocent, for she had not stood up in protest at the blatant disregard for such a fundamental Christian tenet as the sanctity of life.

She bowed her head in shame. She had been too busy protesting about other things: Bibles for those who were denied them and the freedom of the press in its full sense of all printed and published work. Though she could argue that those too had their part to play in the prevention of war, now that the dead confronted her as her accusers, could she deny that she could not have done more, that she could not have tried harder to make her quiet voice of reason heard above the mercenary shouts, the greedy cries and the selfish screams?

She fled the ruins to escape the tumultuous voices of the ghosts and ran to the walled park nearby, hoping that beyond the wooden garden gate she would also escape the tumultuous recriminations of her needless guilt. Instead, she found vision rather than blindness. Her pace slowed to a walk along the tranquil banks of the gentle stream which ran between the unkempt lawns and the mature trees. Her thoughts slowed too, bringing the accusations back into perspective. Yes, one could always have done more, said more, campaigned more, fought more; but that was in the understanding of hindsight. No, she had not acted differently, nor had she acted super-humanly; and for that she had to admit responsibility; but to admit any further guilt was to waste thought on things which could not be changed. Better for her to get on with living in the present and with putting things right in the present to prevent a recurrence in the future. Such evidence of her repentance would be far healthier for her mind, her soul and her body than for her to embitter her future with the by-products of unredeemed regret.

She walked beside the oblong pool beneath the skeletal branches of the beech and chestnut trees, and prayed for divine guidance for that day and in the future, humbled by her own smallness and her failures to do aught to save her homeland from its fate. The spring sun shone weakly through the billowing white clouds and the budless black branches like a witness to her pledge to the Author of the Universe. This city, this country, this world, this star system were little indeed when measured on the scale of creation; yet she would not allow that image to limit her concept of God with the false belief that God was therefore too busy to hear her prayers or too remote to accept her service. She knew that such beliefs were born of that false humility which conceals the inflated pride of the believer in thinking he alone was the only one who could control himself and his fate; and her homeland had been destroyed through such pride.

Her thoughts were racing. She forced her mind to halt the torrent and returned to her car to drive on south.

The Minister had insisted she take the car after his death, despite her concern about the glaring disadvantage of its bright red colour. The small car had been well protected in his garage, and its tank was still three quarters full. She coaxed its reluctant engine to start, and steered it down the other exit of the roundabout to continue her journey south.

At one time she had driven regularly along those broad main roads during their busiest periods. Now they were deserted and eerie. The little red brick houses on either side, once so well cared for, were now crumbling and unloved, their neat gardens neglected and the trim hedges dead. Half way up the shallow hill the traffic lights at the crossroads were blank. She drove on slowly round the roundabout of dead roses and took the turning for the next local suburban town centre.

A tight feeling of fear began to rise in her throat and chest. Her mother too would have been at work that other morning, managing the children's home there. She dared not think the rest and drove on in deepening pessimism, any flippancy about her parents' survival gone.

Her fear sapped her concentration and warped her sense of direction. She drove aimlessly round the town centre for a while, looking for a road she recognised. After some time, she thought a turning by a car park looked more familiar. She drove down the narrow street and found the large dilapidated building she sought, situated in its own grounds at the far end.

The dowdy old red-brick building housed the charitable children's home her mother had run. It was still standing, although neglected long before the bombs had fallen, and repeatedly the target of professional as well as amateur vandals. The bright childish artwork gazing down at her from the windows was faded and brittle – brave reminders of a symbol of hope to so many abandoned children at one time, a symbol which her mother and others had had to fight to keep though it had been funded a century earlier by the bequest of an industrialist in a charitable trust. The property had been more desirable to some local politicians than the good work which had gone on within its walls.

Money! she thought impatiently. Wherever she had gone before the war the cry had been money; the criteria for continued existence had been cost-effectiveness or financial viability or economic sense. And where had all the saved money gone to? Had it been invested for the better prospects of the homeland? No: most of it had gone out of the country to pay for a few rich men's palaces in warmer climes abroad. The economic watchword passed by the monetarists was but another synonym for self-interest, the latest pseudonym for greed. Little indeed of the saved capital had been re-invested in the homeland. Had it been spent there on useless decoration or better sewers or more books, at least it would have benefited the unemployed and the economy of the country which had generated the savings, instead of the unemployed and the economy of some other country which then demonstrated the folly and shortsightedness of such investment when its growing industry outstripped the investors' own.

But what did all that matter in the end, she asked herself sharply to brake her thoughts again. Whether the people who had left this home and shopped in this centre had been employed or unemployed made no difference now to them or to others for they too were all dead. They had placed their dependence on the security of bricks and mortar in the concrete desert for a better existence. She, like Shana Daly, had not; and she like Shana Daly had survived. They had shunned the unreal world of the city, preferring the humbler life of the country where the contrasts between riches and poverty were not so great. Living far away from where all the country's major decisions were made, they had easily been able to ignore those decisions and the dissensions they often caused elsewhere, easily able to get on with daily living without getting involved in anything more than their own pet causes, hobbies and charities.

That had seemed to be how the capital had wanted the provinces to be, too. How the capital had liked to make decisions which ignored the provinces' presence and special needs. In return the provinces dutifully ignored the capital's decisions and had got on with trying to service their special needs as best they could. It had not always been like that, of course; but it had always been hard to remind those fifteen million that there were another fifty million elsewhere in the land for whom they were standing proxy in the decision-making processes.

Such resentment was merely more wasted thought, she reminded herself. The bombs had changed all that. The Minister had said the capital was deserted and all the major towns and cities had been hit. The total population of the whole country was now no more than fifteen million, if that. How many little children like these had also died? Behind each wooden door down the long dim passage with its heavily polished linoleum floor, was another silent room with little piles of dusty clothes amongst the low furniture. Little children who had not asked for nor chosen their roles, lay dead amongst the crayons and the paints, their mortal futures finished, their spirits graduated to the immortal school.

She turned away from the open door into the main playroom, hearing the voice of a friend from the past.

'Makes you wonder if there is a God at all, doesn't it, Katy?'

She spun round, alarmed to hear that name superimposed on that memory. The speaker was not the spirit of the past acquaintance, but Smith. He stood in the shadows of the hall, wrapped in a dark grey mackintosh which emphasised his heavy build. She sensed that his words were a gibe about her three days' rest in the sanctuary of the church.

'Only if you blame God for man's misdeeds,' she replied.

'Oh, but I do. If there is a God of love, why did he allow such suffering here? What did those orphaned children do to deserve their fate?'

His defiance made her recall her defiant reaction to the Minister when they had first met. Perhaps as she had been, Smith too was asking in all honesty and genuinely sought an answer despite his tone of voice. She gave a second more considerate reply to his first question.

'I have always believed that God in the wisdom of God's love, gives us the freedom of choice to do whatever we want. After making a lot of mistakes in my life and going through some really tough times because of them, I chose to give my life back to God. But others have not. Where God is not invited in, satan quickly takes command; and those who believe they sit on the fence are torn in two like I was, gripped by indecision; either that controlled indecision where they grit their teeth and muddle through as best they can, which is what my father did; or that uncontrolled indecision where they swing from mood to mood and court insanity, which is what I did. One day I came to the bottom of my hell hole and I realised I couldn't save myself. So I asked God to help me, and God did. But not many people go through enough to ask that, and not many people choose to be actuated by God. So shouldn't we be more surprised that more bad things don't happen? For it's satan who has been in day-to-day control, through those who allow the devil in; and satan has ever sought only to destroy.'

Smith laughed derisively.

'What, a big horned man with a long tail and a toasting fork? No-one believes in the Devil now.'

She nodded with a wry smile.

'Just because few people believe in satan now or the power of evil, doesn't mean that they don't exist. It just proves how cunning satan is; for the green satyr with the toasting fork is his work, not God's. Jesus was quite aware of the evil one, the prince of this world, and warned all his followers against him.'

Smith laughed again in contempt after tricking his prey into such self-betrayal so easily.

'You can say all that and still claim you are the photographer Kath Brown?' he asked.

His accusation caught her out. Fearing for her identity and her life, she swiftly bluffed a starchy retort to save herself.

'Of course, if you still claim to be my employer. Give me my cameras and I will get on with the job. What is it to be? Pictures of a thriving city to fool the hayseeds back on the farm?'

Her rebuttal contradicted what Smith thought he had discovered. His manner changed abruptly.

'What brought you here? A rendezvous?' he snapped.

His anger roused only her compassion. She looked at him with pity to see how like her father he was in his inability to be greater than the role he played in life.

'No. I came here to bury my mother,' she said.

The quiet force of her unexpected reply took him aback. He could not believe her explanation to be true because it did not accord in any way with what he believed was the truth.

'Why? Was she one of the conspirators? Was she murdered here in some secret meeting?' he blustered, unaware of how he sounded.

She almost laughed at his pathetic attempt to keep himself in the right, but restrained herself. She could see how serious he was and knew that he could choose to be very dangerous. Forcefully she refuted his wild accusations with a calm statement of fact.

'No, Mr Smith. My mother is Eleanor Baylis, the Superintendent of this home for fifteen years or more. On the morning the bombs struck she would have been here in the home, either with the younger children or dealing with the administration. I am searching for her remains in the hope that I don't find anything, that she was off sick that day or something; anything in a way rather than that she is here, dead. And yet, I want to know; I would much prefer to know: rather than not know I would prefer her to be dead. For I have seen what else she could be.'

The transparent sincerity of her reply wrong-footed Smith and convinced him to believe her.

'That's fair enough, then,' he said abruptly. After a short pause he walked off, back out of the building.

His watchful presence dominated the corridors long after he had gone. Though she could not see him she knew he was watching her still. She stood in the passage waiting for his spirit to leave, preferring to grieve privately if she had to; but the shadow of his presence would not go. Regretfully she abandoned her wait and slowly climbed the stairs.

Her mother's office was situated at the front of the building and led off the first half-landing. She paused briefly with her fingers on the door handle, steeling herself for what she might find on the other side. With strength from God she knew that she could walk through all her fears. She turned the handle and pushed open the stiff heavy door.

There lay her mother across the desk, her body desiccated but whole; with her secretary nearby. The colour drained from Sarah's face: she swayed and caught hold of the doorpost to steady herself in the first impact of shock. Then she sat down on a vacant chair with caution, some furniture like some buildings having been weakened through the emissions from the bombs. Her mind was stunned. She kept thinking that this could not be, that her mother would have been too clever to be caught like that. But the fragile face on the desk told her differently, and the clothes and the wristwatch agreed; that distinctive small gold watch her father had given her mother after one of his few trips abroad without her. Her handbag was lying open beside her body on the desk as though she had been looking for something in it at the moment the bomb went off up the road.

Sarah wept. She had thought that she had run out of tears to cry when she could face a playroom of little bodies and not flinch; but this proved her wrong. It was not better to discover for certain that her mother was dead. She would far rather have found nothing there and been able to continue to live in hope. There had been so much unfinished business between them which would never be completed now, such as telling her mother how much she loved her and appreciated all that she had done.

Sarah had not been aware of how much she had taken her mother for granted, until the rigours and the empty hours during her captivity gave her the opportunity to reflect honestly. They had not been close in adulthood for various reasons, unimportant reasons now that she was looking at her through the veil of death. She saw again the happy things, the things she had tried to concentrate upon during those tedious hours and weeks in solitary; such as her mother's chocolate cake, rich and sticky and filled with all the tasty traditional ingredients so bad for one's health. She remembered again the day that they had made one together. She remembered her twenty years later, nervous but adept chairing a meeting, her face holding that same look she had had when refereeing the arguments between her husband and her daughter. She remembered her asleep in an armchair after dinner, and playing Scrabble during long winter evenings; and sitting at Christmas like Juno with children rather than peacocks at her feet. And she remembered her quoting her grandmother's words of regret at the start of an earlier conflict, *So your youth will be spoiled by war too.*

Sarah rebelled against the evidence before her.

'No!' she screamed, leaping up to punch savagely into the air in defiance of fate.

Nothing happened to change what was there. A little dust fell. That was all. The discharge of her grief and anger changed no courses in the divine plan. She sat back humbled in the chair and looked across at her mother's crumbling body, wondering what she should do. The answer came that she should take her mother home.

She looked out of the window at the bright red car she had come in, parked on the drive. To her dismay, Smith was sitting at the steering wheel. Deciding she could not continue her journey in that car, she chose instead to get her mother's small maroon hatchback running again after two years of idleness.

Some time later she returned to the house with a can of paraffin she had found in the garage, and a large cardboard box to hold her mother's remains. When she tried to move her mother's body it crumbled away to powder in her embrace. Crying with grief, she placed the residue of dust and the clothes and the wristwatch and the handbag in the box. Then she sprinkled paraffin about the room, picked up the box in readiness to depart, and threw a lighted match down upon the carpet. Her intention had been to make the home a funeral pyre for all those poor children who had died there, for as the Minister had found, she could not bury all the dead. The room exploded into flame. She fled, escaping only moments before the whole building caught alight and became her pyre and her mother's too.

She leapt into the maroon car and nursed it into movement out of the garage onto the side street. The car juddered awkwardly until the handbrake freed itself, and then shot forward. She brought it to a halt at the first road junction and looked back, expecting to find Smith ready to give chase in the red car. Instead, he was peering through the windows of the building, looking for her in the blaze. He turned and caught sight of her car as she drove out of view round the corner. Alarmed, he wondered whether she or another was at the wheel of the maroon car, departing in haste after an aborted rendezvous.

Sarah left all thoughts of Smith behind to burn in the flames. She was taking her mother home, back to her father, the right place for her mother's remains to be. Once more she headed south down the main road towards the motorway and the coast, running parallel to the railway track across the downs. As she drove, she remembered how lost her father would have felt without her mother. Had he been able to, he would have found her body and taken her home himself. She turned right at some dead traffic lights three miles further south, facing the probability that her father was also dead. The tight tension returned to her throat and chest as she turned left again onto the residential avenue where they had lived.

Even the evergreens had died back, she noticed as she drove along the once attractive avenue. In the car, she was unable to see the first new shoots starting to push through the leaf mould beneath the dormant trees. In years past at that season the avenue would have been pink with cherry blossom. Now the gaunt trunks and naked branches reached out their spindly fingers; their nascent buds still not visible from the road. Half a mile further, she turned the car onto a drive and drew up outside her parents' home. Using the keys in her mother's handbag, she garaged the car to hide it, and let herself into the elegant detached house.

The stench of death hit her the instant she opened the inner door of the porch. She steeled herself to enter, knowing what to expect from the fetor, and followed the smell through the house to her father's body.

He was lying where he had fallen in the lounge two years before, hardly recognisable through decomposition. The rank smell of decay had been trapped in the hermetically sealed house, unable to escape. Sarah hastily threw open the windows and went outside into the back garden for air. Then she found a spade in one of the garden sheds and began to dig a shallow grave.

Sarah buried her parents shortly before sunset, reciting the funeral service from the Book of Common Prayer over them, having found a copy in their bookcase. As she filled in the grave over their remains, a feeling of loss and emptiness washed over her which she was too stunned with shock to identify. She went back inside, determined not to brood on the tragedies she had discovered that day.

The rank odour had almost gone from the house. She lit a log fire in the open grate in the lounge to draw in more fresh air. In the kitchen she opened some tinned food and emptied the contents in saucepans to heat up a meal, but found that the electricity and gas supply to the oven and hob were not working. She turned off the mains and instead cooked her meal over the fire. After some warm food she finished her repast with the treat of a good cup of tea, and looked forward to the prospect of a strong cup of coffee in the morning.

Soon after dark she retired for the night by candlelight, choosing to sleep in the guest room rather than the bedrooms her parents no longer needed. When she extinguished the candle, memories came flooding back through the darkness, filling her thoughts with regret, keeping her from sleep despite her exhaustion. She sensed she needed to come to terms with her parents' deaths and the changes in herself and the world before she could face that house and handle those memories with confidence. Shock weakened in insidious ways, and her wayward thoughts warned her that she must still be in shock. At length she slept. In sleep her emotions healed a little and the shock began to earth gently away.

CHAPTER 10

Sarah woke next morning soon after dawn. Her waking rescued her from a nightmare generated by her mind in its attempts to come to terms with the past. Yesterday flooded through her thoughts with instant clarity. She threw herself out of bed to occupy her mind with opening curtains to let in the new day. Her eyes glanced down from the windows of the master bedroom and happened to see the double grave in the back garden lawn below. She froze momentarily. Then she broke down at last and wept.

Her tears were not shed solely in grief but also in release, for she had been a captive long before she had been imprisoned abroad. Her father had been the unwitting jailor who had locked her in mental cells with emotional keys. She had not realised the roles she and he had played until those lonely hours in solitary confinement had given her the opportunity to review from a distance those parts of the past she could still remember. They too had had a lot of unfinished business left to complete, and she felt cheated that he had been taken from her before she had had the opportunity to prove the truth of their relationship. She felt sadness for her father that he had gone to his grave without having come to terms with his own past sorrows and guilt. And she remembered with pity the often childish man whose public servant double-talk had so confused her all her life. He had only been as childish as all people were at times; and the Civil Service training ground had taught many more people than him how to speak the truth to tell lies. He had passed that skill on to her too, but somehow despite her mental agility he had always managed to keep her one step behind.

No longer would his mortal presence impinge upon her life; but that would not prevent his influence from continuing to modify her conduct. She imagined throwing off his leaden armour to fly as herself at last. The prospect seemed daunting. Without him she felt an apparent vulnerability which was false. He had offered her little protection from any real threats, and even less support in any real battles while he was alive. His manner had forced her to develop her psychic ability in her attempts to hear the truth despite what was being said and to protect herself when no-one was there on whom she could depend.

She checked her thoughts to stifle that ungrateful self pity which always tried to surface when she examined her relationship with her father. Such thoughts bred self-destructive emotions. She discarded them and set about finding breakfast. If she was not yet capable of analysing their parent-daughter relationship in an adult way, she needed to set aside such memories until her mind had healed more and she could.

Yet despite all her resentments and regrets, she grieved as deeply for her father as for her mother, such grief for them both that she felt unable to do anything because nothing seemed worth doing anymore. She returned to their grave after completing the mundane chores of the morning, and knelt on the dewy grass to mourn and pray. Beyond her sorrow she sensed her spirit being borne up on strengthening arms. She looked with her other vision and perceived a cloud of believers from the communion of saints gathering around her there to support her, as a similar cloud had supported her before when she had knelt at the family grave in the local churchyard as a young adult and asked for guidance.

After that dramatic answer to her desperate lonely plea for help, she had tried to understand what manner of power endowed her spirit. Her faltering description of the vision was beyond the interpretation of her local parish priest. Then a chance meeting with a venerable pastor in a neighbouring parish enlightened her. He had reassured her that her psychic vision was not a manifestation of insanity because she was able to control it. The only danger lay in the times it resisted her attempts to control it, because then she was being controlled herself by elemental spirits possibly from the far side of death.

During her first three days back in the homeland she had been stepping in and out of insanity while she had stayed in the heart of the capital. The demon-like block on her spiritual capacity had taken away her natural psychic ability to oversee the astral link which automatically protected her consciousness and her sanity. The drugged cigarettes had worsened that effect. By the third day she had unconsciously started to oversee the link again as instinct strove to protect her from injury. Her healing at the church had seen the return of her former skill. The images she had received since then had been psychic alone rather than psychotic: she had gained a certain control over them again, as she was able to now.

Storm clouds were building up above the skyline. The daylight had turned a murky yellow, colouring the winter grass an unnatural saffron. The struggling plants shrank back into the ground, sensing a winter storm when they thirsted for spring showers. She too sensed danger, of a different sort, and hurried back inside the house. The city had been calling to her, warning her to leave; but until that moment she had been too bound up in her grief, too engrossed in her yesterdays to hear the insistent today.

She changed back into the khaki clothes, sensing she might need their protection, and threw some tins and useful items into a travel bag and a rucksack. She tossed the bags into the back of her mother's car – her car now – and backed the car out of the garage. After locking the front door and the garage she stepped back to check that the front of the house looked the same as she had found it the evening before.

'Good morning, Ma'am.'

She spun round to see a man clad in army khaki with the rank insignia of a major, standing on the pavement outside the front garden. Despite his pleasant tone she sensed instantly that he was dangerous. In her alternative vision he was a wolf in a sheep's fleece. He was not what he appeared to be at all, and she needed to escape him.

'Who are you, Officer?' she demanded.

He smiled and advanced up the drive towards her with his right hand outstretched.

'I am Major Donoghue.'

'Get off my property, officer!'

He stopped, frosty faced, and placed his hand on the butt of the revolver holstered at his waist.

'All city property is held in common bond by the army at present, civilian. Show me your papers!'

She brought her papers out of her top pocket and walked towards him down the drive. For a moment she thought of trying to escape him in the car but realised he would shoot out the tyres to stop her. Closer to him, she could scent the justification for her concern. His body odour did not accord with the man his accent and uniform claimed him to be, but rather with a man brought up on the peasant cuisine of the other side. He smelled like the prison warders she had first learnt to hate and fear.

He leafed through her papers. 'So you are Katherine Brown. Where are your cameras?' he demanded.

She held back a retort and gave him a cold warning to save herself from more trouble.

'I think you ought to know that we are being watched, Officer. My employer considers my work important enough for me to warrant special surveillance. If you have been lured here by the smoke from my fire and you've moved out of your authorised zone, you will be disciplined.'

'I asked you, where are your cameras!'

His uncompromising manner could easily ignite her anger should she choose to allow it. She glared thoughtfully at him, her head held high, her nostrils flared. No, she decided; it was not worth risking a showdown with a man as dangerous as him. She backed down and relaxed her stance.

'I will drive you to them,' she said.

'I do not wish to see them. I wish to know where they are!'

He slipped her papers into his pocket. When she did not answer he drew his revolver and aimed it at her.

'Let me into this house,' he ordered.

'I would not advise that. I also burned down that children's home just up the road yesterday,' she bluffed in warning. 'Propaganda!'

She emphasised each syllable of the last word by saying it so slowly that it turned into a contemptuous threat. He looked at her, then at the house, and then back at her.

'Open the car. All the doors.'

She obeyed. She knew the car could easily be replaced with her father's car, standing in the other garage. However, she was concerned that the Major might drive off without returning her papers. She did not believe Smith would corroborate the Major's threat even if he was by chance watching them both at that moment.

The Major climbed into the passenger seat and ordered her to take the wheel. When he was satisfied all the doors and windows were shut he softly told her where to take him.

'Drive to the motorway. Drive south.'

She started up the car, praying silently. This problem was better left to the care of her Higher Power to solve, for God was far greater than the man beside her as well as herself. She reversed the car out onto the avenue and drove through the residential area back to the main road, heading south.

Still she saw no people on the pavements or in the streets; but as she drove out of the city basin into the countryside, she began to see some birds, and a few signs of animal life. Some touches of bright green gilded a copse of deciduous trees still clinging to life. Nature was fighting back again as nature had always done. The tide of destruction was already turning even this close to the margins of the dead capital.

They came to a roundabout over the orbital motorway, and

found all the slip roads blocked except for the two leading down to the main carriageway. Sarah circled the roundabout while her passenger made up his mind whether to go east or west to continue travelling south. She could feel his concern about the diversion and wondered whether he would instead tell her to drive north back into the city.

'Go west,' he ordered tensely at length.

She steered the car down the slip road on to the westbound carriageway and joined the motorway. The road surface beneath the wheels was dirty and cracked, and winter weeds were growing along the hard shoulder. She drove slowly, fearing that the car might suddenly fall through a crumbling bridge, or collide with an obstacle blocking the carriageway, or shake itself to bits running over the damaged tarmac.

He made no comment. Most of the time he stared moodily out of the window at the views ahead and to the side. Occasionally he glanced at the rear view using the vanity mirror in the passenger's sun visor. At length he seemed to come to some decision within himself. He broke off his vigilance and took out a pack of cigarettes.

'Smoke?' he invited.

'No thanks. I don't,' she said.

'Then what are those stains on your fingers?'

'I used to smoke, when I was in....'

She faltered, realising that she had been about to give herself away. This officer from the other side might be trying a different approach to discover from her what the interrogators had failed to learn and what Smith also wanted to know.

'In prison?' he finished for her.

'No. When I was a captive. Today I am not a captive.'

'We are all captives!' he scoffed, and lit a cigarette for himself.

'If we choose to be,' she agreed, and rolled down her window to dispel his smoke.

The car rounded a sweeping bend. Ahead the motorway was

blocked with wooden beams, forcing all traffic to leave the carriageway by a slip road up to the roundabout above. Two army privates stepped off the verge and signaled to her to drive the car up the slip road. She obeyed, aware that her passenger was not at all pleased.

The slip road exit was blocked at the top by an army unit which had taken over the whole of the roundabout above the motorway. She stopped the car at the roadblock and turned off the engine. Two armed corporals marched over to the front windows of the car, one on either side. The one on the Major's side had to knock on the window before the Major wound it down.

'Your papers, please,' the corporals requested.

'The Major is holding mine, Officer,' she replied.

The other corporal asked him for both sets of papers. He played for time by trying to pull rank. The corporal politely reminded him that he had powers to shoot anyone who refused to produce his papers, even a brigadier. The Major scowled and handed over the Katherine Brown papers to keep the sentry's attention while he looked for his own. The corporal glanced at her papers and handed them across the car roof to his colleague who also glanced at them and nodded in recognition. The corporal on the nearside opened the passenger door.

'If you would like to step out for a moment, Major Donoghue: the usual formalities,' he invited.

The Major realised from the way he had been addressed by name, that the woman beside him had told the truth when she had warned him she was under surveillance. He climbed out of the car in defeat and was escorted by the corporal to the sentry box. The other corporal handed Sarah back her papers for Katherine Brown.

'We were given a message for you, Miss Brown, from Mr Smith,' he informed her: 'He said he would discuss the matter of the children's home with you later, when he catches up with you.'

She smiled and pocketed her papers, glad to have such proof that Smith could indeed be her friend, and a very powerful friend at that, with the army's backing behind him.

'John loves paying attention to detail, thank heavens. And thank you too, Officer,' she said.

He slapped the roof of the car twice and signaled for the barrier to go up. She started the car as the bar was raised and drove through the gate out into the freedom of the countryside. She had left the capital at last.

CHAPTER 11

Two hours after leaving the capital behind Sarah was totally lost. She had so little idea of where she was that she could not even use the map in the door pocket beside her. She had seen no civilians to ask the way and had come across no road signs whatsoever. Her own poor memory of the southern country roads gave up completely after she had driven round in several circles because of a plague of recently constructed artificial dead ends. At length she stopped the car to save wasting fuel and got out to stroll through the extensive birch woods she found herself in, to help her clear her thoughts.

The air was cold and damp after a recent hail shower, and vibrant with birdsong. The budding branches of the birch trees were still dripping, and the brown scars on the trunks contrasted darkly with the silver parchment of their bark. The wet peaty turf was firm underfoot and tufted in places with healthy clumps of long wiry grass. The scrub even showed the marks of deer having passed that way. She strolled on into the recovering brush in carefree appreciation of the visible signs of rebirth all around her.

Through the trees she spotted a tall electrified wire mesh fence topped with a barbed wire overhang. She stopped in alarm. That type of fencing she had seen before as standard construction on the other side. But which other side, she asked herself with unexpected uncertainty. Three sides had been involved in the war, and three in her imprisonment: the khaki, the blue and the grey; the homeland, the allies and the other side; and they had all been enemies of the homeland, and they had all been enemies to her.

She stalked cautiously through the undergrowth, keeping parallel to the fence and peering through it whenever a view appeared between the trees and the fence posts and the barrack buildings beyond. At length she was able to identify the camp from a unit of blue-clad troops parading on the square: the camp was a base for the allies. Despite all they had done, they were still on homeland soil, she thought indignantly.

Their presence there justified her fears and proved the validity of her concern that the full truth was not yet known about the war. Surely the homeland would not have tolerated the allied bases on its soil if it had known the part the allies had played in the diplomatic tangle which had ended up with the bombing of the homeland cites by the other side.

She stealthily returned to the relative safety of her car to consider over lunch the import of what she had just seen. The meal was a simple affair, cold baked beans forked straight out of the tin, leaving her mind free to rearrange all the evidence she had so far found, in the light of such a surprising new discovery.

Was this national lack of knowledge the reason why divine providence had made each of the three sides involved spare her, she wondered. Was it also why Smith was taking such care of her? The way he had organised the homeland soldiers to arrest the spy major from the other side, suggested that he was an influential government agent. His message about the destruction of the children's home suggested that he was also her friend. That would make her indirectly a government agent too, inasmuch as the government was assisting her while it still suspected she had knowledge it required. That knowledge had to be to do with the political story behind the bombs, she thought; but even she did not know the full story about that yet, despite what Smith and others might believe. She might perhaps be able to learn the full story from them and to redeem herself through the use of her alternative perception, if that was God's will for her and for the homeland. In the meantime she decided she should put her differences aside and try to befriend Smith. She should also try to be less hostile to any strangers she met, in case they also had information which could be useful to her.

At least her homeland was still governed by its own, she thought. The country was not yet a dependency of the other side or occupied by grey-uniformed troops; and the allied forces on its soil were still kept behind their electrified barbed wire. The homeland, like herself, was self-governed still.

She stood her empty baked bean tin in the passenger footwell and picked up the map again. After some time, she managed to identify her location, about three miles from a rural village.

'Get out of the car!' a man challenged outside.

His allied accent and his bellicose manner made her automatically unobliging despite her alarm. She slowly placed the map on the glove shelf and looked up at him to see her fears confirmed. He was wearing the blue uniform and bucket helmet of the allied forces, and he slouched with his hands hooked in his belt ready to unholster the gun on his hip. Was he allowed to treat the homeland as a colony of his country, she wondered, or was he overstepping his authority? Sensing danger from this meeting, she did not obey him but instead wound down her window and leaned out.

'Is this the way to the village, Officer? I'm lost. I've been driving around for over an hour, and you're the first person I've found to ask,' she said.

'What were you doing in the woods, lady?' he demanded.

She showed him the empty tin of beans with a smile.

'Answering the call of nature. Even better than playing patience for making people appear out of nowhere.'

'Why are you travelling to the village?'

'To see if any of the family are still there.'

Family meaning God's family, she rationalised inwardly to avoid the admission that she had lied.

'Move along then!' the soldier ordered.

He stepped aside as she started her car. In the rear-view mirror she was horrified to see two other allied soldiers standing nearby with drawn machine guns. She drove off in fear and did not relax until she had turned a corner putting them out of sight. Then she demanded of her psychic power why she had not sensed their presence during the exchange. The response shamed her. Her acuity had been dissipated by her fear and the falsehood in her rationalisation. How easily had her house been divided against itself. She drove on slowly to the village, chastened.

The village proved to be one of those picturesque places popular in calendar and chocolate box photographs. Black and white timber-framed houses with thatched roofs gathered unevenly around the village green. She checked the psychic record and perceived that the villagers had deliberately maintained the image before the bombs for the benefit of the men in the allied camp up the road who had plenty of money to spend on such romanticism. Two years after the bombs, the real stood out from the sham. The quaint little flint and mortar church in its circular graveyard and the cramped chemist shop still appeared rustically sturdy beside the crumbling patchy general store and the neglected house next door.

The village inn looked like a hybrid, with a squat solid basic structure and a dilapidated extension. She parked her car outside the inn and stepped out to look around. When she tried the door to the bar, it opened. Heart racing, she walked inside. She stopped abruptly in amazement, the door swinging shut behind her.

The bar was lit by daylight coming in through the two windows and the warm glow of a log fire. Behind the counter, the plump barman stood polishing a glass, with hand pumps to one side and a few imported bottles behind him. Two customers were sitting at the window table near the fire. They broke off their conversation to weigh up the newcomer.

'Good afternoon, ma'am. What can I get you?' the barman asked.

'People, real people!' she gasped in joy.

'Sorry, I can't serve you any of those. I'm only licensed to sell alcohol, more's the pity, or you could have tried a pint of

Allied blood.'

'At your prices you bleed them to death through more legitimate means!' joked one of the customers.

She spun round, recognising the voice at once, though she had never met either of the customers before.

'Stephen! I knew you and Dougan would still be alive!' she exclaimed.

The two men stared at her in astonishment as they tried to remember who she was. Both men were dressed in civilian clothing suitable for the country: moss green jumpers and quilted jackets with an expensive pedigree. The older man, Dougan, was lean and grey-haired; the younger Stephen had sandy hair and a more athletic build. When neither recognised her, Dougan took the lead.

'Those are our names, ma'am, but I must confess you have the advantage of us.'

She faltered, seeing through his quizzical smile to the snake which was his image within, and then through his younger companion to the image of a wild dog. Confronted by such dubious psychic company she gauged the levels of their spirituality as columns of light emanating through and above them. Stephen's level barely reached his heart. Dougan's level went off the scale, reaching like a pulsing silver pillar into the sky, a dangerous sign when even a spiritually whole person like the Minister had had a golden column reaching only about a foot above his head. She placed the remarkable chance meeting in God's control and prayed for divine guidance to tell her what to say and do. The prompting quickly came.

'The museum park, the eve of the war,' she ventured. 'Stephen expressed a desire to urinate on this democracy.'

Her forthright translation of his sentiment took Stephen aback. Not pleased, Dougan sent her a psychic warning to desist by returning her power upon herself. She winced with the brief sharp stabbing headache paining her behind and above her ears.

'I rather sense you are taking advantage of us now, Mrs....'

Dougan said carefully.

'Brown, Miss Katy Brown,' she answered, quieter but undaunted. She placed herself within a halo of blue-edged white light for protection and continued, 'You told Stephen off, Dougan. You also asked him whether he would be at the south coast rally that night. How did you know to get out of the capital?'

'The same way that you did, I expect, Miss Brown,' Dougan replied.

'I think not. I was elsewhere at the time.'

'Then how did you hear what we said?' Stephen challenged, thinking that he was pointing out her betrayal of herself. 'Even your car's from the capital – I can tell by its registration number.'

She smiled archly, sensing an opportunity to get them out of a place that suited Dougan and into a place that suited her.

'I was wrong. You aren't real either. You're like puppets,' she said provocatively.

She turned and walked out, knowing that they would be bound to follow her to answer the riddle she had set. She crossed the road and strolled up the steps through the lych-gate into the church graveyard. Sanctified ground was home territory to her, and she hoped it would also give Smith adequate cover to listen in to the rest of her conversation with the untrustworthy spiritualist as she tried to learn more about the brief war two years ago. She sat down on a wooden bench by the flinty graveyard wall. The graves opposite her were marked with memorials to people who had died or been fatally injured in that war. Even this pleasant country parish had been touched by that withering wind.

The two men soon joined her. They sat down on the bench with her between them as they had done in the museum gardens, Dougan on her left and Stephen on her right.

'Who are you?' Dougan demanded.

'I have already answered that,' she said, and added, 'I used to be a member of Tony's.'

'Oh, there!' Stephen exclaimed, relaxing visibly. 'The back room passcode?'

'*Just knock three times and ask for Joe,*' she sang with a wry smile.

'That was the passcode at Tony Moreno's?' Dougan asked with amused contempt.

'We students always liked to go over the top,' she said. 'I was back there last week. The red check tablecloths and curtains, and barman Michael's secret cache of house red still there beneath the castor oil plants. All crumbling away, of course: shoddy stuff anyway. It wasn't the same. The city is dying, you know.'

'The city is dead! Evacuated!' Stephen said.

'You miss my meaning. The city may be empty but it is still a collection of buildings; and they are dying also. The hotel I was in collapsed.'

'Really? Did something hit you on the head?' Stephen said.

Dougan leaned forward to caution Stephen with a wave of his hand, and turned an enquiring smile on Sarah.

'Then the authorities must be allowing civilians back into the capital now, Miss Brown,' he said.

She gave him an arch smile to encourage him to believe that she had not had permission to be there.

'No. I was a "special case".'

'How did you get in and out past the army road blocks?'

'I was accompanied by a government agent on the way in, and a spy disguised as a major on the way out. Neither of them said who they were working for.'

'And they helped you for what?'

'I had some unfinished business and a man to see.'

'Really?'

Dougan's tone conveyed his disbelief and contempt. She realised she was moving on dangerous ground with such a man while she was following her father's example of being less than honest, and changed tactics again. If this man was at least as psychic as she was, he would only be convinced by the truth. Moreover, he was used to betraying others: he would expect her to betray him in return.

'Look, I know you don't know what to make of me,' she said: 'But know this: I believe the so-called aggressors were the aggressed, and I want to know for certain; because I already know our land betrayed itself and continues to do so. That camp up the road proves so: foreign forces; armed soldiers, who even challenged me to find out why I had stopped to look at a map!'

Stephen looked significantly at Dougan who narrowed his eyes in return. The young man impatiently stood up, thinking her trustworthy and wanting to ignore his friend's warning glare. He stepped across the gravel path, turned abruptly and walked back, his manner contrived as though he knew the power of his good looks on women like Sarah who were slightly older than himself. He posed for her, his right foot playing on an edging tile bordering the path as he looked out over the older part of the graveyard, his jacket open and his hands in his trouser pockets. When he nodded a few times in preparation to speak, Dougan recognised his moves and quickly spoke first.

'Betrayal is a weighty word, Miss Brown. What good would it do you to know all that?' he asked, his cold tone warning her that it would do her no good at all.

'That doesn't come into it. I simply want to know,' she said.

Stephen's vanity would not let him keep silent any longer when his testimony could win him this haunting woman with the large dark perceptive eyes.

'We thought we were doing the right thing when we supported them. We never thought that they would be the first to drop the bombs,' he confessed, looking away. 'After all that peace and security talk we knew that no-one would go nuclear any more – no-one wanted to destroy the whole world to destroy their enemies. We never thought that they would use that form of attack – they had always claimed they would liberate the people, not kill the people and save the property.'

She looked thoughtfully at the profile of his face against the grey skies, and perceived he did not fully believe his own words. Dougan realised what she was thinking and spoke to undo the damage caused by Stephen's confession.

'As I am sure you understand, Miss Brown, the things we thought yesterday were yesterday's thoughts. After the night of fires, now is what counts, the survival of the fittest, getting by today. I'm sure you understand.'

She turned sharply to look at him, resisting his attempt to hypnotise. His reference to a book on symbolism by Harold Bayley had given her a significant key to the puzzle. She was surprised at the sort of writing he made reference to so casually. To test him, she referenced a similar work, concerned about the total to which his points of character were adding.

'You mean, we were a sacrifice, to appease some lesser god with this golden bough?'

He smiled thoughtfully at her, recognising that this young woman dressed in khaki was far more dangerous than he had first calculated her to be.

'Yes. I mean, the other side sacrificed the homeland to silence the allies,' he said.

'After the allies had indicated the appropriate sacrifice to make!' Stephen pointed out indignantly.

She looked back to him, quick to take up his statement before Dougan silenced him again.

'So you do believe it too, Stephen; that the aggressor was the aggressed. What convinced you?'

'The same things as you, of course,' he said, less confidently.

'But you don't have the aura of a person who can read the Akashic Record.'

'Only because some people are more privileged!' he said, affronted by what he thought was a social snub. 'Where is this record kept?'

'Stephen,' Dougan cautioned to stop him showing off his ignorance but stopped speaking himself when she answered the question with neither condescension nor contempt.

'In the Earth's etheric.'

Stephen turned back in astonishment, his face clearly requesting the explanation he could not ask of her because of Dougan's previous censure. Dougan chose to enlighten him, seeing an opportunity to elicit more information from her.

'Miss Brown is a mystic, Stephen. She refers to a Buddhist concept I believe, a form of spiritualism. But you are not a Buddhist or a Spiritualist, are you, Miss Brown. You would not be here asking us all these questions if you were.'

'All things are possible, Dougan, if God wills them.'

'You mean, your God willed all this?' Stephen demanded, gesturing to the graves to indicate the war.

'No, the allies desired that, and the other side granted them their wish,' she sharply returned. 'So why don't you tell me, how did you know to leave the capital that day?'

'We didn't,' Stephen protested, quick to deny the betrayal her words implied. 'We were out of town by chance, at that rally on the south coast you mentioned, a political charity do, you know the sort of thing.'

More pieces of the puzzle slipped into place for her. Stephen had been out of the capital by chance, but Dougan had not. She turned again to look at Dougan, and remembered the foyer of the doomed hotel a week before, as the photograph came into focus on the front page of the newspaper held by the tailor's dummy. Dougan's was the face that had illustrated the headlines with his talk of peace and security: he had been the politician most keen to advance that public cause; and he was the snake who had privately betrayed that cause. His psychic image was not the snake but the Serpent, the Deceiver. His spiritual level was not that of an erring spiritualist but a satanist, one who for his own selfish ends was a follower of the Destroyer. In him the Evil One had won the perfect servant to further his destruction, and no man of God had had faith enough to unmask him or to oust him from power.

'You are not what you appear to be at all, are you, Dougan,' she whispered, her voice low and trembling.

He seized upon her faltering faith and projected images of evil into her alternative vision. She leapt up with a cry of fear and ran for the church. Demons of hell flooding her perception drove her to hammer on the massive oak door. When the door did not open, she turned at bay, expecting to see Dougan's menacing face right behind her.

Instead, she saw Smith standing inside the lych gate, his left hand in his raincoat pocket. With his prosaic appearance the demons instantly vanished. He touched the brim of his hat with his right hand and gave her a brief smile of reassurance. Then he strolled along the path to the two men at the bench.

Stephen was still standing with one foot on the tiled border, looking back at Sarah in surprise. Dougan was still seated, arrogant and contemptuous. Smith spoke briefly with them. He did most of the talking, and most of his talk was an apology, which they appeared to accept in good grace. He thanked them and walked away to where Sarah was still standing, at the church doors.

'Come along, Katy. I'll take you for that drink,' he said loudly, so that they would hear.

He linked his left arm through her right and patted her hand. His voice dropped to a whisper.

'I told them you were on a day out from the asylum up the road. I apologised for you and told them not to worry.' Then raising his voice again, he spoke as though he was patiently replying to a comment from her: 'Yes, and then we will go on to your Auntie's like we promised.'

He gripped her arm so fiercely that she winced with pain, and forced her to leave the graveyard before the army moved in. As they strolled out he sent Dougan and Stephen an exaggerated smile of sympathy-seeking embarrassment.

'But I am not insane,' she muttered through clenched teeth, totally unable to resist Smith.

'That's neither here nor there: you're getting too close to the truth,' he replied, and forced her across the road back to the inn.

CHAPTER 12

The barman was still standing behind the counter polishing a glass when Smith marched Sarah back into the bar. It was a good vantage point, giving the barman a clear view through the left window of the incident in the graveyard. Smith realised this from his expression and took care to seat Sarah at a table with her back to that window so that she would not see what happened next outside. He asked her what she wanted to drink and ordered two soft drinks at the bar. The barman took the order with an expression that showed he thought the sale hardly worth dirtying the polished glasses.

Smith leaned back against the bar to wait for his order, appearing to stare at Sarah as he watched through the window and saw Dougan and Stephen being arrested. The barman handed him the two drinks with a knowing scowl. Smith nodded back, dropped some coins on the bar in payment, and took the two glasses over to the table. His mind was turning over Sarah's conversation in the churchyard and the barman's interpretation of her actions in the light of everything else he had seen.

'Katy, you're getting a bit too morbid for my liking,' he said. 'Whenever I look, you seem to be in churches or graveyards or burying the dead. Fixations like that aren't healthy. You're even beginning to sound 'not normal'.'

'But that's precisely what I am, Mr Smith: 'not normal', paranormal. Or may I call you John? If I were normal, you would not have employed me as your photographer. People who genuinely believe in a God who is both transcendental and immanent at once, are not thought of as normal in the eyes of the world; or at least that part of the world which only lives for its senses.'

'But Katy, there isn't anything else. Those ladies in their

tents at the seaside fairgrounds with their cards and their crystal balls were just shamming. And you call yourself an adult, yet still you believe in them!'

She looked away from him down into her glass, a reflective smile playing across her face. The homeland used to pride itself on its protection of the freedom of speech; but this insidious unofficial censorship was just as dangerous to that freedom as the overt state censorship practised by the other side.

'Do you know why the other side arrested me, John? I was smuggling in Bibles. They tried to convince me that there isn't anything else too. I thought at least back home in this country I would be allowed to think and say and believe in what I like.'

'Not when it means burning down a children's home in a pointless wish to cremate a handful of the millions dead. We have all been through a hell of a lot in this country in the past two years, Katy. You are not the sole queen of suffering here. We're coming to terms with it. We're getting on with life, starting afresh, rebuilding the nation.'

'That may be true for many, John, but that is not true of you or of *Now!* Magazine – you are totally bound up in yesterdays. The sole purpose of our relationship is for you to find out what happened yesterday, and the yesterday before that, and all the yesterdays before then. Do you know what that man was who I was talking to just now, before I realised I was walking on water and my faith failed me?'

'Yes, thanks to your conversation with him, I do,' he hedged, knowing that the barman was listening.

'Is it not now apparent that he was a lot more than a pure traitor?'

'He was a member of the Opposition, Katy.'

Her laugh belittled his polite protest.

'Yes! He was actuated by satan, John! 'By their fruits shall ye know them.' Look what happened despite the peace talks he attended – they were bound to fail. There is a simple rule of thumb, more often true than not: the God of good creates and upbuilds; the Devil of evil undermines and destroys.'

'If you ask me,' interrupted the barman unasked, to save Sarah from her folly and the threat in Smith's expression: 'The easiest rule of thumb is what you live by, you'll die by. The city people got themselves too enamoured of this modern technology, so what happened? This modern technology up and killed them, every man jack. And life goes on without them, ah, and without that modern technology too.'

He patted his large stomach.

'And John Barleycorn is what I'll die by, I don't doubt; but there's worse ways of dying and I've enjoyed myself with this one. You, young lady, ought to watch the company you keep. And you, sir, should mind you're not in uniform now. And here come the first of the boys off duty from up the road.'

A jeep drew up outside the inn. Five young men dressed in blue uniforms strolled in through the door, laughing and joking in their distinctively accented form of the homeland tongue. Their eyes glanced lewdly across at Sarah, seeing another potential sex object for the games they would not play back home. She recognised their looks and hastily finished her drink.

'I must be going,' she said abruptly, and rose to her feet.

'I'm coming with you,' Smith said.

He did not waste time finishing his drink. With a curt nod to the barman he quickly escorted Sarah out to her car. She climbed in the driver's seat. He joined her on the passenger side. She looked at him with a mocking smile.

'Are you going to protect me from the five young bucks? Or from the satanist and his apprentice?' she taunted.

'Neither. The young bucks will not be permitted to follow us; and the two in the graveyard have already been arrested, on the strength of their conversation with you. We still live in an emergency state.'

'Or a state of emergency,' she absentmindedly corrected his verbal shorthand.

His news of their arrest surprised her. She had not thought

the authorities would act so decisively. Sensing that he had joined her in the car for a reason, to see who she next met up with on the road, she asked him for directions. He confirmed her fears by leaving the decision to her. She asked him to tell her the road north and started up the car. He checked the road map and pointed the way to go.

Why had he not asked her to justify her journey, she wondered as they drove on in silence through the homely spring-touched countryside. Meanwhile, he thought about the discrepancies in her story while he waited for her to start justifying herself to him of her own accord. Some time later, after several more directions north, she began to relax.

'I'm glad you're being a bit friendlier now, John.'

'That is only because you're being a bit friendlier too, Katy; nothing more than that.'

'I'm sorry, John. I simply didn't know whether I could trust you until this morning and the incident with the spy.'

'You shouldn't have mentioned him to Doug Chandler, not even in passing; and you certainly shouldn't have mentioned me. I always had some reservations about that power-disdaining little extremist; and for all your fanciful notions you did agree with me there. He would have been arrested before, you know; long ago, only we couldn't find him. I'd thought he'd been lost in the fifth bomb. I was wrong. You led me straight to him. Quite a coincidence!'

'God-incidence. Stick around me long enough and you'll get a bellyful of them. What really made you suspect Chandler?'

'Surely you wouldn't expect a government agent to tell you that,' he teased.

His expression became more serious. There was a question he had been waiting to ask her as soon as he was certain she had recovered from her partial amnesia. He began with an opening gambit to draw her attention to all the discrepancies.

'Especially not when you claimed to have met Chandler and his side-kick in the capital the evening before the war. Who are you really, Katy Brown?'

She thought about the question as she drove, around another bypass around another town. Should she bypass his question too? He should have worked out who she was for himself by now from the jigsaw pieces she had already given him: her mother dead at work in the children's home, her father dead and decomposing in the parental home, her former school and the academy, and the Bibles in the tour bus to the other side. He would have access to official records: the information to answer the question would all be there. Then why did he demand that statement of the known from her? Was it disputed elsewhere? Was another woman living by the name of Sarah Baylis, claiming her life and her past?

She knew at once that that was what had happened; that she needed to re-establish herself as Sarah Baylis and prove the authorities' error, or be known for the rest of her life as the photographer Katy Brown. She mentally compared the two identities and listed all the things Sarah Baylis had that Kath Brown did not: faith in something greater than political dogma, an ability to sketch and paint, a friend called Shana Daly, somewhere still perhaps a dog called Bubbles Kamir and his canine friends, a psychic gift which sometimes allowed her to see into the secrets of the universe. Only to her friend Shana Daly would the difference of name mean anything. Why then had someone taken over the identity of Sarah Baylis and left vacant the identity of Katherine Brown for her to fill?

Kath Brown herself, she thought: a straight swap. They had known each other quite well, well enough for them to go on that trekking holiday tour together with eight other friends; well enough to step into each other's place, perhaps? Certainly they had looked similar. Even Kath's latest boyfriend had not been able to distinguish them from behind when they had been trying on jackets in a little village shop they had stopped at during the tour.

She recalled the details of that fateful tour. She had only

taken a place on the bus by chance, after one of the girls had been forced to drop out because of divorce proceedings. Café Annie had mentioned the spare place to Sarah when she had stopped off at her coffee shop in town as usual one Saturday. Café Annie had known that she had not got enough money for an independent holiday that year and had been quick to suggest her name when Kath Brown and her brother Darren had come in complaining about the last minute cancellation.

Darren Brown had made all the arrangements for the tour. He had been a capable young man with no self-confidence. He had kept saying that the trip was the first thing to go in any way right for him, and that her faith had saved the trip from his organisation. As they were the only unpaired people on the tour they had teamed up amicably with little in common but enough holiday good will to get by together for three weeks. Had he known about the Bibles she was smuggling, he would have laughed it off as a bit of a joke or praised her for finding a good money spinner. He had understood her precarious finances and paid many of her incidental tour expenses without asking for any money back. She had wondered at the time whether he had contrived to get her along on the tour because he wanted a girlfriend like his sister. The realisation of the truth dismayed her. Darren had rather contrived to get her along on the tour at his sister's request so that she could exchange places with her.

But why? Still Sarah could see no motive. She sensed she would need to go home to find out. There she would be able to discover whether her circle of friends considered her missing or dead, or whether someone else had taken her place and her name. When she had those facts she could better answer that question why.

'Who are you really, Katy Brown?' Smith repeated.

'I don't think I'll answer that just yet, John Smith. The time is not right. Other things need to happen first.'

'What if I am not prepared to wait?'

She shrugged her shoulders, sensing that the threat in his

question was not backed by intent.

'How do you know I'm not Katy Brown? *Who do you say that I am?*' she asked.

He smiled at her device and parried it with ease.

'I've read that book too, Katy. I say 'I do not know' and you say 'neither will I tell you'. So why were you smuggling Bibles to the other side? Surely you knew how foolish that would be?'

'You know what young people are like, Mr Smith,' she said wryly. 'I was barely past my mid-twenties, still had some rough edges to rub off my idealism. It was all a bit of a lark to me. I wouldn't get caught, not with God on my side!'

'So why did you get caught?'

'Maybe God thought it was time I had a lesson in humility. Pride always was my weak point.'

'If that's Divine Providence, I think I'll stick with the basement department. You know, the "have now pay later" brigade.'

She scowled, not considering eternal damnation something to joke about. 'That is your choice, Mr Smith,' she warned sourly.

He struggled not to laugh. The sum of his experience had taught him to accept the whole of existence, including life and death, as nothing more than a wry cosmic joke of universal proportions.

CHAPTER 13

Dusk was falling over the midlands. The evening was damp and misty, and cold enough for a late frost. Smith said it was the sort of weather all the cities had now at that time of year. Sarah nodded and drove on.

Their afternoon's journey had been relatively uneventful, if a little slow because of damaged road surfaces and lack of direction signs.

'Hangover from the last war, that: as soon as there's a chance of invasion, all the retired army majors go out and spirit away all the road signs,' Smith said.

The maroon car topped a bluff in the road and a city spread out below them in the sunset as ridge upon misty ridge of dusky towers and factories. It had once been the first and largest of the midland cities. Now, it too was unlit and unlived in, a ruin like the capital to which it had once played second. Smith asked Sarah if she wanted to stop there overnight to have a look round.

'Who's being morbid now?' she taunted. 'Must we?'

'You need petrol,' he reminded her.

'You are blackmailing me again.'

'Simply trying to influence your decision in my favour.'

'Why? What is there in this city that isn't in any other?'

'Nothing. It is merely the nearest. That is why I want us to go in.'

Such evasion warned her that his reasons were quite the reverse, that he wanted her to find something or someone quite specific in that vast mausoleum spread out below them over so many square miles. He was testing her. She drove on into the city, uncertain that she could perceive anything in her alternative vision when she knew he was waiting on her every move.

The fall of this city had been far more mean and conclusive

than the fall of the capital had been. Its towers lay in ruins in their concrete parks and plazas like defeated dinosaurs in a desert of dereliction and decay. Within the empty outer residential ring lay another belt equally deserted and equally grim, of older buildings of soot-stained red brick tottering beneath gaping roofs of dark grey slate and tile; a workhouse world of tall chimneys surrounded by little terraced houses. Once this area had been a happy place: its past community spirit raised her spirits a little as she drove through heading towards the city centre. The road shortly took her back into another concrete desert, a maze of shopping arcades and places of amusement built solidly enough to have survived. At their centre was a large roundabout. She halted the car at the give way line.

'Why have you stopped here, Katy?' Smith asked.

His manner told her that he had not wanted her to stop there. She drove on, ready for his next indication.

'I didn't mean that we had to go on. I only asked you why you stopped there,' he said.

'I only paused for directions,' she replied.

She took the third turning off the roundabout because of the way he became more tense as they neared it. Fresh tyre marks on the road caused her to turn again almost immediately into a small side street which led straight to a large modern hotel. She drew up under the hotel portico and switched off the car's engine.

'Remarkable! Precisely where I wanted us to be,' Smith remarked genially.

Anger flashed up inside her: she struggled to control it as she unfastened her seatbelt and took the key out of the ignition. They stepped out onto the pavement, and she paused to lock the car.

'Yes, someone's really going all out to impress with their psychic gifts, aren't they!' he said, mocking her caution.

'Stop putting me to the test! It doesn't feel right!'

'Why? Doesn't it work when we get out of our depth and

into the real world?'

She realised too late that he was trying to goad her into self betrayal, and bit her lip to silence another retort. Before she answered him she walked round the car and joined him outside the hotel's plate glass doors.

'My psychic ability works intuitively rather than to order. The pressures of testing weaken it significantly. It responds to other pressures, and many of those it responds to very well.'

'Pressures such as the threat of death?'

'Keep your petrol!'

She turned sharply back for her car. He caught hold of her arm to prevent her from leaving.

'No! Wait, Katy,' he ordered

She turned again and looked him straight in the eyes. Confusion and dismay hid behind his facade. He was prowling like a trapped cougar, pained by his vulnerability. But what circumstances had trapped him into this unlikely relationship with her – more twists in world politics to find a new whipping boy, perhaps; or simply to catch another spy? She pulled her arm free of his grip.

'What, am I meant to fear you? The Bible tells me to fear only those who would destroy the soul with the body, not the body alone.'

He nodded thoughtfully and shrugged his shoulders to cloud the meaning of his response. His mouth pulled to the right with a wry expression, as he gesticulated towards the hotel doors.

'Shall we go in?' he invited.

She realised that she could not refuse.

CHAPTER 14

The hotel was silent and in darkness. Smith switched on a pocket torch and walked round the far side of the long reception desk to the control board for the ground floor lighting. Lights came on in the hotel lobby, muted ambers and golds which lent the modern designs a homely atmosphere. Sarah stood inside the closed entrance doors thinking how clean the foyer looked for a deserted building in the heart of an evacuated city.

On the far side of the hall stood a pair of doors which drew her across. She touched one of the doorposts, attuning herself to her surroundings. The double doors opened onto a large ballroom which was in darkness. She paused in the doorway, her foot poised to enter.

'Go in,' Smith encouraged: 'What do you pick up in there?'

'You want me to do your job for you?'

'Of course. I am your employer.'

She was tempted to ask about her wages but decided against the retort. Instead, she entered the ballroom. As her right foot touched the polished maple floor the bright dance-floor lights came on, momentarily blinding her eyes to the circle of tables and chairs around the edge of the room.

She slowly crossed the dance-floor, her footsteps loud and definite on the wood, her senses straining to pick up any nuance in the atmosphere, any indication of past emotion. The information was slow in coming to her consciousness because she was trying too hard. At first she sensed only negative indications: there was no sorrow in the walls, no layer of suffering across that room like the blanket everywhere else in that city and in the capital. Then more definite moods came through, of hard gaiety and false enjoyment: the people who had once danced on that floor had not danced there purely for fun but in the spirit of competition and also the spirit of negotiation. Careers and business deals had been won and lost in that room; lovers' knots had been tied and hearts had been broken. She paused on the far side of the dance-floor. That was the safest room in the hotel, she sensed, and that was why she had felt drawn there.

Smith watched her from the doorway, wondering whether she would notice the piece of paper lying by the leg of a table. She strolled slowly round the edge of the dance-floor, moving steadily towards the scrap but with her attention clearly elsewhere. When she reached it, she surprised him by absentmindedly picked up the paper and placing it on the table without a second glance as she moved on. After she had completed the circuit she walked back out through the double doors into the foyer. He crossed the ballroom to pick up the paper she had moved, and joined her back out in reception.

She was standing at the desk with her back to the ballroom entrance, her hands fingering a bulky red hotel register left at the end of the counter. The atmosphere in the hotel was seeping through into all her levels of consciousness, making her feel unexpectedly low and strange. He could sense her change of mood, but could not identify any reason in the objects around to account for her unease.

'What is the matter?' he asked softly.

She looked down at the book in her hands.

'When can I leave here?' she asked.

'You haven't answered my question. What is wrong?' he demanded.

She sensed he was trying to restrain the imperative, and responded with a precise explanation of what she perceived in those walls.

'The stone tape has been overdubbed. There is a loop beneath which plays back whenever it's triggered by a receptive person. Spirits are trapped here, and though they are dormant their negative attitudes are still powerful enough to influence whoever is here. There is great hatred in this building. It was built in hatred and its opening was marred by hatred and it was run in the spirit of hatred from day to day. Oh, why do these people not realise what they do? Our every passing thought is recorded: not one jot is ever erased from the Akashic Record unless that is God's will.'

Like marionettes the spirits of the haters' souls were forced to act out the loop until the devil freed them to move on to their next existence where he could control them more, or until a follower of God was able to release them from their prison through an act of unselfish love. During their material lives they had ignored spiritual matters for the mundane, and now they were paying the penalty. They had foolishly followed the worldly philosophies of the times and had fallen as desperately as the rest of those masses, each into the hell of his or her own making.

That disappearance of belief in the concept of evil as an active force had been a most worrying sign of the times for her in the months before her imprisonment, for she had known even then that disbelief did not make evil disappear or render it harmless. Though the spiritual powers which fought over those pitiful scraps of the mundane were beyond her imagination to explain, that did not preclude their existence. In the psychic planes everything exists which humankind might possibly imagine, and far more as well, because most of existence is far beyond the wildest imaginings the human mind can create. Even the black and white impossibilities of united opposites have entity there because the planes embrace far more universes than this materially extant creation of atoms and gravity and mathematical logic, replacing the orb and the evenness of two contrasted against the oddness of one, with other logics equally as obvious and compelling. To those other universes the learning spirits of souls travel when released from their existence, and from those other universes they travel once for rebirth in this; and the time they take is not in a straight line from yesterday to tomorrow, but a swirling cloud of inter-related nows to prevent any spirit having a previous experience of the universe to which it travels next.

She had been speaking without realising that she did. Smith was standing back from her in the foyer, clearly displeased.

'This God stuff of yours is starting to annoy me,' he warned. 'When I ask a question I expect it to be answered. I do not expect a philosophical lecture on a concept of good and evil which should be confined to kiddies' shows. Who killed Cock Robin and four-fifths of this nation? The other side. Tough. Let's take out our vengeance on the traitors in our midst, as it's safer and we can be far nastier. Then we get on with the task of rebuilding, and refuse for a while to play ball with the other side again. Maybe it's no tooth for a tooth or just retribution, but it seems like the best way to do it for me.'

'You're sounding very disillusioned, Mr Smith. Even you are being influenced by the loop in the stone tape. Hatred saps all our energy, takes all the goodness out of our systems and leaves only the acid; it pickles our brains in bitterness and starts cancers in our bodies. You too can find instant hell if you want to.'

'Don't you think this country already has?'

She bowed her head, he incorrectly presumed in her deference to his timely reminder. Rather she was trying to pick up some conflicting images which were almost completely being obscured by the powerful wall of hatred. He joined her at the desk, thinking that he should resume the sympathetic approach again before the next item of the evening. Like her, he leaned his forearms on the counter. She looked left across at him.

'I am sorry, Mr Smith: you were right to rebuke me. The answers you expect are in this book. At least, that is what I sense, but I also sense that the answers are wrong. Or is it that I am only human, and I am often wrong?'

He noted her failing self-confidence with interest, knowing

that the entries in the hotel register had been deliberately faked to catch her out. She glanced back down at the register and passed it along the counter to him unopened. He opened the book at the last page of entries and then unfolded the torn piece of paper which she had picked up off the ballroom floor. She looked with interest, recalling where the scrap had been found. It bore some writing in green ink: the initials R.S.V. and the numbers 3.3.0 beneath.

'What does that mean, if it's not a reference to a reserved special vintage?' Smith asked.

'It could be several things: a reference in the Revised Standard version of the Bible, perhaps, or a torn off request for a reply, R.S.V.P. It could even be a message for me,' she said. 'Are there any entries in the book in green ink?'

He checked. There proved to be two, both on the two pages uppermost. The last entry had been written in fresh-looking emerald by a Mr Eric Constantine from the north and was dated about three months ago, long after the city had been evacuated and surrounded by the army. A more faded green entry five from the end had ostensibly been written by Sarah Baylis of Dubmill Kennels a little more than two years previously, during her imprisonment on the other side.

'Why do you think this message might be for you, Katy?' he softly asked.

She looked at him with frightened eyes.

'Because I used to write in green ink, with a fountain pen. But I did not write these,' she said.

'I know. I was watching you from the ballroom door. Do you know this Eric Constantine? His address appears to be near the border, where you're heading.'

His last phrase sounded as though it had been tacked on as an afterthought to cover a mistake. It made her wonder whether he already knew who she really was.

'Can we leave now?' she asked flatly.

He shook his head and held up two sets of room keys by

their tabs. She looked at the room numbers on the tabs and nodded thoughtfully.

'Fair enough. I'll leave alone. And before you mention it, I do know how to get hold of petrol in a city like this, at a pinch.'

He smiled wryly and pushed a set of keys along the counter to her.

'What good is petrol without a car, Katy? And how will you get out to look for it?'

She turned in concern towards the main entrance and saw with dismay the empty street outside the plate glass doors where she had parked her car. She ran over to try the doors but found as Smith had warned, that they were locked.

Their visit to the hate-filled hotel took on a completely different meaning to her when she found herself trapped inside its cankerous environment. In panic she pounded her fists ineffectually on the doors until she dropped exhausted to the floor, sobbing.

Smith watched her impassively from the counter. After she had stopped sobbing he crouched down beside her and touched her left wrist in reassurance.

'But Katy, you knew yourself that you're a prisoner still. I heard you say as much the day after you got back. No matter how free you may appear to be, it is only an illusion. You may have the choice of accepting your position in good grace or throwing yourself in anger against the bars; but you cannot change the prison: you can only change yourself.'

She glared at him, red-eyed, implacable.

'And how long must this go on? Or is this sentence for life?' she demanded.

'I honestly don't know, Katy. You see, I'm a prisoner too,' he said.

His transparent sincerity startled her. She had not considered that he might not be happy in his work, because his training had been so thorough that the role appeared natural to him. She watched him tensely, waiting for his next move. After a moment's reflection he continued to speak.

'You know, you ought to consider yourself fortunate: at least you have a heaven to look forward to. I take the same risks; but I have nothing.'

He placed his right hand beneath her shoulder and helped her to stand up.

'Come on. I'll take you to your room,' he said.

CHAPTER 15

In the quiet of the night the hotel began to speak to Sarah. She lay in bed and listened to its whispered resonances, her hands on her hips as she rested on her back. Her single hotel room was in darkness, a comfortable modern bedroom with en suite bathroom and little furniture. Net curtains hung across the plate-glass window wall, clean billowing net as white as the crisp cotton sheets she lay between. She luxuriated in this cleanliness: it was a quality all too rare in the regions of the bombs.

The bedroom was a quiet peaceful place: it had long since assimilated what little disturbances had been caused within it by the hatred breeding in the hotel. Its walls assured her that the past trapped in the loop of the stone tape could not harm her now, but it gave only fleeting impressions of what that hatred had caused in the past. To find out more, she began to travel in her astral body through the hotel corridors until she found a place where the original stone tape would play back for her. She found the place she sought on the ground floor.

The psychic activity was centred around the general office, but even there the metaphysical record only gave illustrative scenes of the personalities involved, no indication of how the hatred had begun. Two people had been involved: a short plump, balding man wearing a dark green cardigan over a grey and white striped shirt and a pair of well-loved brown-green trousers, whose back was always turned; and a slim, attractive middle-aged woman with neatly styled auburn hair who wore either a green cardigan, white blouse and brown trousers, or a brown skirt and a reddish-brown polo-neck jumper. The relationship between the couple was a little hell of venomous hatred which had so entrapped them that neither had thought to walk away from such destructive habits in search of a better life and a more loving relationship elsewhere. Yet the walls which confined them to such a prison of an existence and the ties that bound them together were manifest only in their actions. These demonstrated that however tenuous their links might really be, they both believed themselves to be helplessly confined there and eternally bound together.

She had learned that difference in prison: the difference between believing herself to be trapped by circumstances, like those old Monday morning feelings, and the physical reality of imprisonment when the door was locked behind her in the bare box-like room. Both could make a person pound against the doors, though only in the cell was that protest rational, because prison warders could hear. To combat the frustrations of a mundane existence she had used prayer.

She had found God always heard her prayers and welcomed them. God always responded too, though not always immediately and not always in the ways she wanted. Her prayers were always answered, many of them despite her doubts, and often beyond her furthest expectations, for she had often made the mistake of putting human limitations on her perception of God and had not thought in terms of infinite wisdom and divine abundance. Yet one of those answers had been that extreme punishment for a negligible offence, a long imprisonment in the hands of sadistic warders which was far more severe a penalty than the smuggling offence had deserved.

For months she had paced that austere cell and glared at the chipped paint on those stone walls and raised her fist at those black bars and shouted at those unbending jailers. Why, she had demanded, forgetting to ask the other five questions as well: who, what, when, where, and how; the six serving men of understanding. In youthful indignation she had failed to see her own wrongs and wasted herself in needless suffering as she protested her innocence. She now saw how she had let pride separate her from God. The consequences of that error followed as a matter of course.

Yet God had seen fit to use her imprisonment as a means of saving her from death and disfigurement, and for that she had cause to rejoice. Her sentence had prevented her from being anywhere near the target countries on the day of the bombs, or the night of fires as the former politician Dougan Chandler had referred to the war.

She reconsidered his turn of phrase, recalling the noticeable absence of burnt-out buildings in the empty capital and this empty city. Had his literary allusion been only as deep as the idea it conveyed of sacrifice? Still that did not explain the complete absence of fire. The cities had apparently been struck soon after the working day had begun: even if the blasts had consumed all the immediate oxygen, machinery would still have been running, vehicles driven, heaters and fires still on. Did the power fail everywhere at once too, or had everything been cleaned up afterwards? Were the cities required for new people now? Had she been wrong about the causes of the war, and had the victors been wrong about the damage to the city structures through the bombing? Could a new solution for those miles upon miles of semi-dereliction be for them to house the homeless of the world? She smiled cynically: no, even after facing annihilation, the homeland's leaders would never become as altruistic as that.

Her thoughts returned to the building around her, the hotel with the tragic loop in the stone tape beneath the devastation of the bombs and the deep hatred built into its foundation. This city structure was sturdier than the rest, but only because it had learned to withstand loneliness earlier, for in hatred there is always loneliness and isolation and hunger for love. Few other buildings if any in this vast dead city would still be as solid and as sound as this hotel.

That was why the meeting had been held here, in the ballroom the previous week, she remembered with the building's complacency: she could not possibly have known that herself as fact. The walls continued to feed the details as images into her subconscious. The meeting had been attended by leading administrators forming a new government, who had chosen the hotel as the venue because of its sturdiness, its centrality in the country, and its proximity to the motorway network. A few participants from the northern kingdom had asked for the meeting to be held in another major city further north, but the rest from the body of the homeland were well-used to ignoring such requests. Some had even hoped that shortage of fuel would prevent the nationalistic upstarts from risking such a long journey south.

It had been a fiery meeting, all the more so without the restraining presence of the new King. He had not been invited to come, lest his enthusiasm to help his nation should infect the more practical administrators with less than egocentric motives. Altruism could upset the delicate balance which kept the organisation running for the benefit of the politicians in charge. After all, why else did a politician bother to stand for election and do all that voluntary work?

The hatred in the hotel's foundations had inculcated her too, she realised, as it had the administrators at that meeting and everyone else who had stayed within those walls. She was relieved that the beneficent King had not attended the meeting to be touched by that hatred too, and suspected more God-work there, more divine coincidences. It had also been good that the meeting had been secret enough to keep out the Doug Chandlers of the country, the people whose one clear aim seemed to be to complete the destruction in the land.

She caught her breath sharply, reminding herself that that was not completely true: most of the Doug Chandlers of the country were only out for themselves, too short-sighted to see that their deeds could cause complete destruction. The amount of destruction in a human project is proportionate to the amount of selfishness involved; total selfishness causes total destruction. Therefore, it was significant that after two years a considerable part of the homeland was still surviving with more than a semblance of order.

And she lay still in a small bed in another hotel room in another dead city, receiving the recorded transmissions from the stone tape and the Akashic Record; thinking the thoughts that were others' thoughts before her own, and trying to understand their meanings without imposing her own interpretations. The night was far gone and the day was almost at hand. As she put off the things of darkness, for a brief time she slept; until she was woken early next morning by Smith paging her to join him for breakfast.

CHAPTER 16

Sarah entered the dining room with a dramatic pose between the two swing doors to deliver Smith an announcement.

'The meeting was held here last week, John: in the ballroom, just as you thought.'

He looked up at her across the dining room, a reflective smile playing on his face. The bright morning sun blazed through the ruched net-curtained window on his right and shafted across the laden white-clothed table over which he presided like some character in a dated film.

She took the warning from his manner and looked again to see whether he was acting. For a brief moment she saw his alter ego as a dashing young army officer in a peaked cap with an aura of tragedy beneath his youthful spirits, like one who had recently survived a battle in which he had watched his best friend die. The image vanished as quickly as it had appeared. She blinked, disconcerted, and walked into the room letting the doors swing shut behind her.

The dining room looked as though breakfast had long since been served. Most of the white-clothed tables were bare but for their black on white room number tabs. She took her place opposite Smith at his laden table, remarking that she had not seen such an attractive traditional breakfast served in such a good hotel for more than twenty years. He did not seem to hear her appreciative comment. She looked at him more intently and saw as it were a veil draw across his impassive face.

'When did the catering corps arrive?' she enquired.

'You were saying, about the meeting,' he prompted, ignoring her question.

'No, no: after the thank yous,' she said.

She clasped her hands together under the tablecloth and

closed her eyes.

'God wasn't cooking it in the kitchens,' he remarked.

She opened her eyes with a benignly impish smile.

'I'll be happy to thank the kitchen staff too.'

She closed her eyes again, and became aware of other people in the building beside the caterers, people who were watching them both. For their benefit, Smith had assumed the arrogance required for the part others expected him to play. And all of them would be being unwittingly affected by the hatred emanating from the walls.

She took care to link well with God as she recited a simple grace over the meal and invoked blessings on the fellowship and events of the day ahead. A divine serenity seeped through her emotions, giving her a gentle confidence she knew would disconcert Smith behind his act.

She started eating in cheerful silence. Her knife and fork chinked loudly against her plate in the resonantly empty dining room. Smith poured himself out a second cup of coffee. She raised her cup for him to fill that too but he ignored her and set the coffeepot back down on the table. With an indulgent smile she poured herself a cup, shrugging off his slight because she sensed it was caused by the demarcation he thought the people watching wanted to see between them.

'My apologies, Mr Smith. I appear to have said or done something wrong,' she said, sounding not the least bit concerned.

'I am waiting for you to tell me about the meeting,' he answered coldly.

'Oh, silly me!'

Her manner changed instantly. In rapid fire delivery she gave him the information he wanted with a forceful precision which surprised him. All she had seen projected by the walls in the night she now described in words. At least fifty people had attended the meeting in the hotel the previous week, all from different parts of the country. Most of them were men, and the

King was not among them which had led to more informal and forthright discussions. She listed some of the subjects they had discussed and some of the problems and personality clashes thrown up in debate. Almost all of the information she gave was correct to his knowledge, except for two fundamental facts which she had got totally wrong.

'But the meeting is to be held next week. And it is entirely for the benefit of the King, to rally support for his directives. Of course he will attend,' Smith said.

'No, the meeting has already been held; here, in the ballroom last week; and the King did not attend,' she insisted. 'The meeting was deliberately held without his foreknowledge to prevent his attendance; and in my opinion that was just as well: this building contaminates everything that enters it with divisiveness and hatred.'

'Then you must have got your wires crossed, Katherine Brown. The meeting is scheduled for next week, and the army is allowing no-one to enter this city beforehand, let alone this hotel which has been occupied for the last nine days.'

'If you say so, Mr Smith,' she agreed in a tone that clearly stated her personal disbelief. For had the building been occupied by the army the previous night, she would have noticed it during her astral body travels.

She exchanged her empty breakfast plate for a side plate and liberally helped herself to toast, butter and marmalade. A sudden thought struck her. She paused, a slice of toast held up in her hand.

'I hope your army hasn't made this hotel a key building in its strategy for this city,' she said.

'Of course it has: this is the soundest building of its size for a hundred miles,' Smith replied.

'Really! Have you asked yourselves why?'

She set down her toast to make an urgent appeal.

'Mr Smith, please listen to me. This is important. Any plans brought into this hotel are doomed, because this building is cursed. This is a prison of angry spirits of souls which should have moved on. Until they do go, only discord and anger will come out of here.'

He stared at her with an expression of incredulity which slowly turned to scornful laughter. Although she was used to such disbelief, his reaction saddened her because it told her her warning would not be heeded. She would not be able to convince him, whatever she might say or try. Only events would prove the accuracy of her prophecy, if he had the humility to be proven wrong in the metaphysical over the material field.

She made a polite comment about the meal and lapsed into silence as she continued to eat the toast. When she had finished Smith offered her a cigarette in the manner of a peace offering.

'No thank you,' she refused with formal politeness: 'I do not smoke.'

'You did the day I brought you back from over the border,' he said.

'You mean, from the allies, Mr Smith? I didn't know who I was then, and cigarettes were a form of currency to me. I do know who I am now, so I know I don't.'

'Why should that make any difference?'

He lit up a cigarette and inhaled its smoke with a deliberate pose intended to make her crave one. She turned her head away from the temptation and looked out through the netted window on her left into the paved patio with the concrete walls beyond. When he gave up his pose and smoked more casually again, she turned back to ask him a question which had been on her mind since the morning of the exchange.

'Mr Smith, why did you have to buy me back from the Allies? Why didn't anyone buy me back while I was in prison on the other side?'

He sipped his coffee, delaying for time as his mind ran through all the possibilities behind her two simple-sounding questions.

'We hadn't known about your being in prison on the other

side, Katy: we only have your word for that. So far as we knew, you'd only ever been in the custody of the Allied Forces.'

'What?' she demanded in consternation. 'And is that supposed to make it better, my three years in prison – I was with the allies? Imprisonment is the same no matter whose side you're on.'

Smith shot her an expression of disapproval, followed by a statement of quiet force.

'You know that's not true, Katy.'

'Don't make the mistake of listening to your own propaganda, Mr Smith. Imprisonment's the same no matter which country you're in: there's still the locked doors and the pokey cells; and the little room hidden away where official eyes choose not to look. There's still the box of toys not on the inventory; and that's true even for ourselves.'

'Perhaps it was, Katy; but I doubt whether it is now. We don't have the manpower any more. Too many other things to do; too few people to be about them.'

'Then can I go? Leave you to get on with your work?' she asked brightly, concealing her recognition of the half-admission she thought he had let slip.

He smiled at her bald attempt at persuasion.

'Unfortunately, no. I am from a different unit and I have a lot more time. You have done a lot of good work for me: the spy, the anarchist and the rebel, the scrap of paper in the ballroom. I could almost get promotion simply through following you around.'

'Then let me go and follow me. I won't run too fast.'

He laughed at her continued light-hearted attempts to persuade him and shook his head.

'No, Katy. Don't you see yet? If you could lead me straight to them and to this hotel in less than a week, after three years in prison abroad, the details of which we have only your word for; maybe, you're from the Allied Forces; or maybe, you're from the other side.'

'You mean, you've been told to treat me like a hostile agent.'

His head jerked in surprise to hear the turn of phrase she had used. He knew she was correct in presuming that he himself did not believe her to be a hostile agent. She began to understand that her fate was not solely in his hands. The realisation extinguished all her cheerfulness.

'How long must I stay in this building?' she asked in a low voice.

'I don't know, Katy. You have been too accurate about the meeting, right down to the half-errors to make you sound a convincing psychic. But Katherine Brown was not psychic: she was anything but. She was a down-to-earth photographer and a level-headed business-woman with a lot of skills but nothing in the line of sixth sense. Even three years in solitary couldn't turn that material into you.'

'But you don't consider me an impostor, do you.'

'That depends upon the way you mean.'

'Why? What is about to happen to me?'

The unexpected fear in her question alerted him to a rapid transformation taking place in her. The confidence and hope she had regained in a week of freedom, drained away in the face of renewed imprisonment. Her eyes became dull and lustreless, not in defeat, though that was there, but through absence, as though her spirit had vacated her body and gone elsewhere to escape a hopeless fate.

He recognised instinctively that this was not the way to win the information he sought from her; but could he convince others of that? He dabbed his mouth with his serviette and stood up to leave the table.

'Finish your coffee,' he said: 'Someone will take you back to your room shortly.'

He hurried out of the dining room to request a different approach.

CHAPTER 17

Sarah could not complain about her cell at least, she reflected: there were plenty worse prisons than a single suite in a requisitioned five-star hotel. She stood at her bedroom window looking through the white netting at the quadrangle seven storeys below. There was no escape: Smith had chosen the room well the night before. Its modern white walls received her with unusual homeliness as though it felt sympathy towards her for being imprisoned within it against her will.

She swore at herself for not recognising Smith's trap and allowing his persuasions to sway her when she had tried and failed to part company with him the previous day. Then she rebuked herself for such self-criticism - had that trap failed, Smith was able to mobilise such forces that he would only have had to use some other possibly less gentle method to bring her there. As she had given her will and her life over to God's care that morning, there had to be some divine reason for her continuing imprisonment. Therefore, she should accept what was happening with equanimity while she was unable to alter it, and use the time for contemplation and spiritual development.

Although the threat of renewed imprisonment had shocked her, she had recovered quickly because she had moved on emotionally from those arid friendless times of imprisonment she had known before. Through the Minister's healing she was no longer alone. God was eternally present in meditation, her friend and saviour Jesus was always willing to talk with her, and the communion of saints was forever upholding her in the timeless river of faith. Gone was the mental block which had so impeded her spiritual travels before. Gone were the chains which had confined her wanderings to the lowly psychic realms where impish lesser spirits eagerly try to pull down more evolved beings to their own mean level. Once she had almost succumbed to their terrorising images: she could still recall their long fingernails tapping against the barred window of an earlier cell; but no longer did she need to run the gauntlet of their attack.

Her chain of thought raced on to the column of marchers she had seen in one of her early visions while still barely a teenager. The vision engulfed her once more: the endless column ten abreast of all the world's poor and oppressed, marching along the sandy bed of a rift valley, driven on by western overlords in dark uniforms riding black motorbikes. The pounding of the feet and the roar of the bikes had been deafening and disturbing. She had flown repeatedly between the cliff tops and the valley, desperately pleading without effect to end the seemingly ceaseless round of slavery and mastery she saw. There was no stopping the relentless tide of humanity: she might just as well have tried to stop the ocean. Cease it did in the end, of its own accord after uncounted millions had passed; without her having done anything effective to help it cease, and with no side gaining any advantage in their journey through the valley of death.

Fifteen years later in the prison of her hotel suite, she saw how this latest war had ended of its own accord independently of anything she might have wished to have done to stop it. Once again young allied conscripts would have come home with chunks missing from their minds after long months of horror on modern battlefields quite beyond the endurance tests and life lotteries of all those previous 'wars to end all wars'. The lives of another generation were shattered and maimed because of some ideological threat among a nation of people who would rather have sorted out their own problems in civil war, and eventually did.

Then returned that other teenage vision: the cage in the baroque rotunda decorated in pastels and white with elegant niches in the ornately moulded walls. Like a trapped animal she had cowered in a bamboo cage too small for her to stand or sit. Out of the niches vindictive faces pointed accusing forefingers at her while she cowered helplessly, unable to escape the vilification. At length she had released the thongs which held the door, a struggle in itself because of the constant attack. But though she had thought she had managed to escape, she had failed to untie the thongs holding the cage together, and so had continued to carry her prison around with her long into adulthood.

And then one day a stranger on a train shared with her how God loves us, just as we are; that we don't need to do anything to earn God's love; just accept it. The words were a revelation. The cage vanished. The unconditional love of God, described in the life and death of Jesus, smashed forever the unhealthy ties of conditional love constructed by her family. Through her life since, apart from her three years in prison, Jesus had been her constant companion, guiding, teaching, chiding, loving her into a better form of herself.

He was there with her now as he always was, a tall lean man dressed in rough-woven robes of cream and amber, with a tawny face, dark uncut shoulder-length hair and eyes like night. Sometimes he stood beside her; at other times like this he was sitting on a convenient chair, leaning forward with his chin cupped in his left hand and his left elbow on his left knee. Sometimes he gazed on her in compassion, sometimes with his eyes creased in gentle laughter or liquid with sorrow to see her foolish ways. This time his expression challenged her, asking her why she had not thought to talk with him earlier. She apologised for her forgetfulness of him and for her spiritually blinding willfulness which had been born of a misplaced trust in Smith and the fear of facing the unknown alone. His gentle smile told her that she was forgiven.

She told Jesus about the two people trapped in the loop of the stone tape, and asked him to release them from their spiritual prison. Her surroundings changed, and she found herself standing again in the vast white marble hall where she had often brought suffering creatures to God in prayer. Jesus was standing there as before, at the top of three curved white marble steps, with his arms outstretched in welcome. He was robed in white and crowned with thorns, and over his shoulders draped a long blue and white striped chasuble flecked with threads of gold. She bowed to him from afar and guided the couple from the hotel across the floor to the steps. He smiled compassionately on the couple, placed his hands on their shoulders, and told them they would be released from their prison when the time was right for their spirits to be discharged and for their souls to move on. They walked away across the hall and out of sight. She knelt before him on the steps. He raised her to her feet and reassured her that part of the reason for her being kept at the hotel was so that she would bring the couple to him in prayer.

The marble hall dissolved around them until she was looking at Jesus across the darkening bedroom again. Outside the window the sunlight had faded from the quadrangle beyond as evening settled in.

She asked Jesus why she and the couple could not be freed from the hotel immediately. He wordlessly explained that God's creation had laws of cause and effect. As creation is a school for those who will sometime be Jesus' companions in eternity, God's wisdom and justice meant that God rarely chose to intervene miraculously, because the creatures needed to work through the consequences of their choices. The couple trapped in the hotel had created their own prison of hatred, mistrust and fear which had accumulated in the walls until the building had become a vast battery of negative energy. For them to escape, more positive energy was required to cancel out this force. Their fate in this reversal would not be made known to her. Her own part: her compassion and prayers, and her practising trust and faith in such faithless surroundings, could help towards their freedom by supplying more positive energy to counter the building's negativity.

The part she needed to play dismayed her. Could she really risk telling a man like Smith who she was and have any hope of being freed by him when even her name was in doubt? She looked again at Jesus for an answer. His compassionate eyes chided her gently for being tempted to step outside divine providence. Acting contrary to God's way would place her at Smith's mercy, a prisoner Smith could treat however he chose without fear of complaint from his superiors. But if she tried to carry out the divine will, God would give her all the confidence and protection she needed to complete the task, however hard it might be. She acquiesced to divine suggestion and asked for the guidance and strength to do God's will.

She reached out for the room-phone to tell Smith she wanted to talk. As she was fumbling for the handset a key turned in the door. A young homeland soldier marched in and switched on the lights. Blinded, she threw her right arm across her face and turned her head aside to shield her eyes from the sudden brightness.

'Get up! Smith wants you downstairs!'

She quickly rolled off the bed to obey, despite being blinded by the light. She had come across soldiers like him many times before and knew not to give them cause for anger. Bottom of the pecking order in their own hen house, they liked to pick on hostages from others knowing that their victims could not make any effective protest. He brandished his rifle. She obediently put her hands to her head and walked before him out of the bedroom. He escorted her to a spacious single office at the far end of the ground floor lobby with two soldiers standing guard outside the door. They sent her in alone.

CHAPTER 18

Smith was already in the room. He gestured to Sarah to sit on one of the vacant chairs in front of the glass-topped table, and locked the door. She sat down meekly with a bowed head, looking for Jesus' position in the room. He was sitting on the other chair on her side of the table, at the corner by the curtains. He gave her a reassuring smile and encouraged her to open the conversation. Taking her strength from him she looked up to speak to Smith.

'I was just about to call you up on room service when your messenger arrived,' she announced.

Her tone implied a significant coincidence in the timing. Smith kept his gaze fixed on her as he sat back down. He recalled her comment about coincidences the previous day and wondered whether she was trying to engineer this into another one. Her facial expression did not back up that suspicion. She looked far too relaxed to be lying. Nor did she look as though she had been detained all day without food or company or an expected time of release. Somehow she was continuing to thwart his attempts to evaluate her despite his skills in evaluating others. He refused to consider her a special case while there was still a distinct possibility of her being the person by whose name he addressed her. If she was Katherine Brown, she was a skillful operator indeed never to have denied her name to him yet to have made it perfectly clear from the start that that was not her real name.

'I have an apology to make to you, Katy Brown,' he said: 'We have spent the day checking your statements about the meeting here. We found that you were quite correct. A meeting of county leaders did take place in this hotel last week. Some of the details you gave were so specific you could not have guessed them or deduced them from any clues you might have found which we might have overlooked. We also know because of that precise detail that you could not have been told about it beforehand, and we are certain that you did not learn about it afterwards because I have had you under surveillance every day since then.'

'What, even in the church?' she asked.

She blushed, fearing that Smith had overheard her confidential confession to the dying Minister. Smith had not heard that but guessed the cause of her embarrassment. He would have preferred to find her blushes less than genuine to make them fit in with all his superiors' preconceptions about her case.

'What do you expect, Katy Brown? You were handed back to us labelled a traitor, to be dealt with accordingly, yet you claimed you had only been smuggling Bibles. When you wouldn't confess we put you on a long leash and waited to see where you'd run – your sort of traitors always have friends.'

Suddenly she understood why Smith had dealt so promptly with the counterfeit major, the politician Doug Chandler and his friend Stephen: Smith had genuinely believed them to be her friends pretending to be her enemies in case they were under surveillance. She deplored the treachery and deceitfulness of the society in which he lived and was glad that by God's grace she did not have to accept living with such dishonesty too.

'So what did you want to talk to me about?' he asked.

She glanced at Jesus, who gave her a reassuring smile, and turned confidently back to answer Smith.

'I was advised to tell you who I am. By my Higher Power, that is: not someone outside. Jesus explained to me how it's pointless me holding anything back from you now as you are in full control over me in this negative energy battery of a building unless I generate some positive energy by being honest to cancel things out a bit.'

Smith stared at her in astonishment, understanding little of what she had said except that she had received orders from someone during a time when she should have had no contact with the outside world.

'Have you finally cracked completely?' he demanded: 'Who talked to you? And how?'

His lack of understanding saddened her. Though her evidence seemed to be converting him to a belief in psychic gifts, he clearly still had no grasp whatsoever of the relatively simple concept of prayer. She patiently replied with an explanation to ease his alarm.

'God talked to me through God's personification of the Supreme Godhead known as Jesus Christ Emmanuel. We conversed through prayer and meditation. I asked his advice, he gave me it, and here I am in the power of the Spirit trying to carry it out. Why not ask Jesus about it yourself? He's sitting here right next to me at this table.'

She waved her right arm to the corner of the table where she had visualised Jesus sitting at the start of the meeting, and received a smile of encouragement from the Godly observer. Smith hastily declined her invitation to talk to thin air, and ran his hand over his face in confused exasperation as he brought his thoughts back to basics.

'And God told you to say…?' he prompted.

'Nothing. Jesus advised me to start practising a lot more trust, faith and honesty to escape this prison of mistrust and fear and to help others escape too.'

He stared at her in pained astonishment. The more she explained, the less he understood, as though the glass through which he saw clearly in part was being increasingly obscured by the light shining through it. She perceived his confusion and knew that the time had come for her to explain herself to him instead of answering his questions.

'I am Sarah Baylis. I come from the Borders. Until three years ago I lived with my dogs Bubbles Kamir, Princess and Scottie in a cottage in the grounds of Dubmill Kennels, though I suspect you'd call it more of a beach shack than a cottage. Then someone dropped out of a minibus trekking holiday arranged by Kath Brown the photographer and her brother with some other couples. I heard about the spare seat through Annie's Coffee House: Café Annie was always trying to arrange people's lives. I hadn't thought I'd be able to afford a holiday that year – kennel maids don't get paid a lot, and I spent what I could on painting – but this came up and I found I could. Thanks to Darren Brown who seemed to take a shine to me, I had a really good time too: he kept paying my tickets for me rather than see me left out of anything.

'Just for a laugh I smuggled some Bibles along on the bus, which I'm pretty sure now Kath and Darren knew about though they never let on. "Spreading the Gospel", I called it in justification; but you have to watch: whenever you start justifying things with reasonable excuses, you know you've got a motive wrong somewhere. I actually smuggled Bibles for a bit of excitement, to be a "great I" if I succeeded in snubbing the authorities, and what is hardest to admit, to get some cash on the black market. No missionary zeal there. The devil must have been laughing all the way round to his backside over me. And of course I don't know the first thing about smuggling and black markets: I'm an artist, not a bootlegger. Needless to say, I got caught.'

Smith's face was impassive as he listened. At last she was making sense to him: her confession was plausible and gave facts which could be proved or refuted. Previously she had taken great care to give him the impression that she was Sarah Baylis, with her visits to the school, the children's home and the house in the outer suburbs of the capital, and with her references to life while at the Academy, to art and to religion. If her confession was merely another part of the clever act of cunning Katherine Brown, she would soon be caught out now by the detail in her statements. However, if she had finally found the courage to tell him the truth, she should have abandoned all evasiveness and would no longer try to withhold any information.

She looked at him as she paused for breath and realised that though the next part of her confession would beg his disbelief she had no fear of his disfavour. Thrown back on God's strength alone, she was proving again the scripture that when she was at her weakest she was at her strongest through the confidence of faith.

'Between the time of my arrest and the time of my imprisonment several months are missing which I can't yet account for, when all those things would have happened like courts and appeals and involving the embassy, which I simply can't remember. That summer is missing for me. My memories return from that autumn: I was a prisoner in solitary confinement in a cell on the other side, number 1376259, no name. What can you do when you don't speak the language? After a couple of years they exchanged me into the hands of the Allies; but nothing changed except now we spoke a similar language: the sort of rooms didn't change and the type of treatment didn't change. I still didn't know who I was, but when you called me Katy Brown, I knew inside that that was not my name. And I knew nothing about the destruction in our homeland until I woke up in the capital last week and discovered it was dead.'

She paused for him to question her statement. He appraised her story knowing that if she had built him a house of cards, his duty now was to knock it down.

'And this "message to you", the Sarah Baylis signature in green ink in the guest register here, at a time you claim you couldn't possibly have been here because you were in solitary confinement on the other side?'

'That entry was a fake. What way, I'm not sure. I took it to mean that Kath Brown has been pretending to be me for several years, probably ever since I was arrested, so that she could get out of the country in one piece. If you'd let me go after I'd seen that register I would have set off north at once to find out if that is the case; to see whether Kath Brown has changed places with me, and if so, why.'

He noted with interest her correct claim that the entry was counterfeit. However, her explanation was precisely the sort of claim Kath Brown would have said were she the woman there in front of him. He needed to shock her out of her glib explanations. Suddenly he exploded into attack.

'You expect me to believe all that, after all the other rubbish you've been feeding me? Don't make me laugh! Either I get the truth out of you now, or you find out the hard way what we do here with prisoners who don't talk!'

She looked at him with complete calm, knowing from Jesus' assurances that she had nothing to fear as long as she was honest. Only the devil wanted her to fear, and for the moment the devil was using John Smith as his unwitting tool to further that end.

'Stop acting, John. It's pointless trying to act in front of Jesus. He can see right through you, you know,' she chided gently.

Smith leapt to his feet with a roar in a show of outrage. When she still did not even flinch he switched off the act at once and sat back down. He replaced the fury with a conspiratorial smile. Her eyes rapidly moved up and down him as she sought for his true attitude behind the ever-changing mask.

'And why didn't you tell me all this before, hmm?' he asked.

'I was frightened of losing my freedom,' she confessed. 'I feared that if you took the Katherine Brown papers away, I would be left without an identity. You see, until I met the Minister in the church by my old school, I didn't know who I was: I only knew a bit about who I wasn't. Yes, I had memories, but many of them had somehow been overlaid. The Minister channeled God's power which took away the blocks in my mind and made me whole again. The healing brought me out of great darkness, a hole so deep that there was no light whatsoever. He gave me back the light; but by then I was in the habit of walking in the darkness: I'm having to get back the habit of walking in the light again. Maybe this time I'll be more careful not to get caught out by the night.'

He considered her words, his elbows resting on the tabletop, a pen balanced between his fingers. Could such an intelligent, imaginative woman hold such an eccentric, simplistic faith, he wondered; and could such faith see such a woman through what was probably the most traumatic week in her life? He could hardly believe that, but equally he could not believe the faith she professed was the pretence of an impostor. No-one pretending to be a member of the established church would come out with the sort of rubbish she spouted like so much holy verbiage; the insanity of her theistic claims was not the act any agent would use to create the effect of a believable faith. Nevertheless. that impression of a believable faith was what she had created.

And despite all that spiritual garbage, or perhaps because of it and the hint of joy which seemed to be threaded through it, he liked the young woman. This came as some surprise to one who always kept his emotions out of his work. Her religious honesty and the practical nature of her mysticism in the face of his disbelief, prompted him to come to a decision based on intuition rather than judgement. Out of his pocket he pulled the keys to her car.

'You give me enough evidence to put Kath Brown away, and you're free,' he said, dangling the keys to tempt her.

'I have no conclusive evidence; and I will not create any false evidence for you. As it is written, *Thou shalt not bear false witness*,' she warned.

He placed the keys on the tabletop.

'I am willing to negotiate.'

'You mean, no more tricks? Before you were only willing to shout at me.'

'I had to find out whether you were telling me the truth, one way or another.'

He moved the keys further towards her.

'You find Kath Brown and get her to betray herself with her own words, and we will do all the rest. And you'll be free.'

She looked at him in consternation.

'So that is what this has been about all along, is it? My life wrecked completely in three countries just so you and others can nail Kath Brown? Why? What is she supposed to have done?'

'What everyone else says you are guilty of: the betrayal of your country,' Smith said.

His grave tone chilled her. She looked into his face and saw from his expression that his allegation was no joke. Indignant protests clamoured within her, but unfounded pleas would not save her, she knew; however incapable of betrayal she believed herself to be - the betrayal of her parents, her friends, her relatives, her past and her heritage to death in the destruction of the homeland cities. The only way she could prove her innocence was to prove Kath Brown's guilt, to make the impostor betray herself through her own admission of such treachery. No verbal protest of innocence would convince him or any of the others before then.

She stood up and took the keys from the centre of the glass-topped table.

'You have a deal,' she said.

CHAPTER 19

The early morning sun shone with a summer warmth which heralded the end of spring. The sunlight gleamed across the paintwork of her car as Sarah turned onto the main road north and left the city behind. Through her senses coursed the excitement of newly won freedom. She was still not free of responsibilities: those remained, as yet inescapable; but she had gained the freedom of no longer needing to consider Smith a threat.

The evening before, as soldiers had escorted her back to her suite, she had overheard snatches of an argument between Smith and his superior in which Smith had placed his career on the line to gain her release and had won despite the disadvantage of his rank. Though she sensed his belief in her was secondary to his desire to win a greater prize, the arrest of the traitor Katherine Brown, still she did not wish to betray his faith for more reason than mere misplaced loyalty. It was no mistake that he still insisted Sarah should use Katherine Brown's papers, for should Sarah fail he would still have a Katherine Brown to hand over to the authorities. She knew that the people in the wounded homeland would not be so nice about the distinction between the innocent Sarah Baylis and her traitorous former friend as he was being.

The motorway stretched emptily north before her. Only the forces used the motorway network now, she had been told. The army units along her route had been warned to expect her car and would not interrupt her journey unless she needed help or something had gone wrong with Smith's organisation. She had officially been granted the freedom of the open road.

The former main artery of the country disappeared into the distance like the route to release it had always been for her before the night of fires. She recalled those earlier journeys of escape and return which had repeatedly made her run to the capital for mental stimulation only to flee from it again to escape city and family pressures.

Now those pressures were all gone. She drove away from the past, placing distance as well as time between herself and those memories; rejoicing at the prospect of being able to close this latest episode in her life after she had claimed back her identity from the woman who stood accused of falsely and deliberately betraying her into the hands of her enemies. She felt no desire for personal vengeance because she knew to expect such misdealings in life when the same and worse had happened to her Saviour before her. Her desire was to return to the status quo by securing justice for herself: having experienced three years of injustice she did not want to live the rest of her life that way.

To that end, ahead stretched the open road: not endless, of course, but endless it had never been despite the youthful illusions to that effect. There would be new roads to travel and places to explore, but not yet for her: she still had to rediscover the old roads to see how they too had changed in the intervening years and through the events after the night of fires.

The night of fires, she repeated. The phrase still lingered in her head as though it were more significant than a mere euphemism used by a former warmongering politician to describe a catastrophic one-day war. Surely that time had hardly been a night of fires: more a day of bombs, a morning of death, a black Friday. She wondered in passing what day of the week it had happened on, but threw aside the speculation as there was no point in knowing that. It was more important to find out why Doug Chandler had given the day such a name. If he had simply been alluding to the sacrifice without intending any further significance, he must have evaluated Sarah far more swiftly than she had him at their surprise meeting despite her advantage of having met his spirit previously. Only someone fully adept in psychic skills could have managed that. A shiver rippled through her soul at the thought of his black arts, and she took her right hand off the wheel briefly to sign herself with the protection of the cosmic cross of the one true living God.

A faded road sign invited her to turn off to a service station where she had often stopped briefly during long journeys in the past. With pressing business to complete elsewhere she ignored the invitation to break her journey for a needless walk down memory lane. The service station pressed her with the tempting promise of other people being there, but still she resisted the blandishments, knowing that generally only evil and negative things tempted with that much allure. Perhaps some negative parasitic entity sought to feed itself a while on her spiritual energy, not prepared to make the effort to follow the Godly way itself where it could tap unlimited energy from the source of all good.

Rain began to fall. She turned on the windscreen wipers thinking how muddy the rain and the road appeared to be. Then she remembered. A fatal multiple road accident had once happened beneath the service station bridge, exaggerating the psychic veneer overlaying the plain statement in the Akashic Record. Someone caught up in the tangled wreckage of coaches, cars, lorries and tankers had died in such hell that his mind had punched a series of exaggerated negative images into the psychic mantle there. That was why she had always stopped at that service station, she recalled regretfully. She threw out the images of hell from her alternative vision and placed Christ there in their stead. The wrecks shimmered into vapour and the red rain dissolved away. She turned off the protesting windscreen wipers and drove on.

The carriageway verges along the six-lane motorway were so overgrown with rampant weeds that the crash barriers were all but engulfed. The neglected road surface was scarred with deep potholes, which forced her to slow down and drive vigilantly.

This rapid return to disorder through neglect was part of the natural order God had built into this universe to bring it from its inception to its death. Death had a rightful place in the scheme; and she at last was also beginning to fear death, just as the rabbit did as it bounded across the road ahead of her car to escape the hawk hovering high above them in the clear blue sky. Though fear signified wavering faith, the fear of death was a natural emotion which also had its rightful place in the scheme. She played briefly with the fear until adrenalin flowed through her arteries again and she remembered how unpleasant it felt, after three years trying to prevent such physical reactions to survive captivity.

She returned her whole attention to driving along the road. A grey shadow began to pervade her alternative vision with a distressing sense of loneliness and aloneness. To counter, it she pretended for a while that nothing had changed while she was away, that the cities and her parents were still there as they had always been, like a safety net beneath her isolated life in the country, always available for her to escape back to should things go wrong. The artifice did not satisfy.

Now she had only herself and her own resources to rely upon in worldly terms. In such weakness she had to rely instead on God, whose omnipotence and infinite resources were far more dependable than her own.

Yet still that grey shadow of social failure cast gloom in her senses and across the land through which she was driving. All society's former dependables had gone, and with them the old order. The lost remnant needed to find new dependables and a new order; but the shock of losing so much so unexpectedly had left the grieving survivors unable to distinguish between what was firm and what was unsubstantial, leaving them lacking sound foundations.

When she realised the encroaching shadows were made up of others' fear and despair, she fought to throw off the oppression, for she could not let such negativity undermine her own soundness of mind.

She turned on the car radio, hoping to pick up some local transmission as she drove on across country between the silenced midland cities. The auto tuner failed to pick up any stations, and when she tried the manual tuner she only picked up two foreign stations broadcasting long distance in languages she did not understand. Though she had failed to hear any homelander transmissions yet, she found some comfort in knowing that other countries did still exist besides her own, the allies and the other side. She left the radio switched on and tuned to the former national magazine programme bandwidth, with the volume turned right down so that the detuned noise did not annoy her too much.

Ahead of the car rose the graceful arc of the mile-long road bridge lifting the motorway over the once vital road, rail and canal links between the capital of the north and the city port on the west coast. Always a progress marker on her past journeys, this day it signified that she was half-way home from the hotel, and two-thirds of the way home from the capital, but still with the hardest part of the journey ahead.

The bridge was already breaking up. Chunks of concrete had fallen away from the sides, taking with them parts of the inside lanes and the safety rails. The remaining fabric was cracked and potholed. Her body tensed as she drove cautiously across on the middle lane, praying the bridge would hold, knowing there was no other way round. Economic policies had denied the provincial roads their rightful maintenance even before the night of fires. Had those who governed yet learned to stop their conjuring tricks with the national product? Fearing not, she slowly drove down the far side of the span, and heaved a sigh of relief as she came back safely onto solid ground again.

The factory belt to the north of the bridge lined her route in stony silence. Unadorned modern buildings designed to please the eye with structure alone were crumbling and rusted in abandoned defeat amidst encroaching weeds and brush. Those survivors who had once enlivened this centre of industry had gone away with far more important business to do than mass-produce unwanted consumer goods. The logo of a sports equipment manufacturer stood out on one of the factory walls. She wondered briefly whether anyone bothered about sport any more.

The road seemed less damaged as she drove out of the factory belt. Her thoughts began to explore the important interview which lay ahead. She sent the six serving men into action: how should she approach the meeting; what should she expect; where and when would it take place; who would she finally unmask; and why did a woman she had thought a friend play such a cruel trick on her? Dismayed to find the serving men did not automatically act as a team, she had instead to marshal them as their commanding officer for them to serve her to her best advantage.

She started again with the question who, and came up with a more complicated answer than she had expected. The person she was going to visit, Kath Brown, was wanted by the homeland army. Its representative John Smith had persuaded her to force Kath into self-betrayal. But the woman had not betrayed herself before, either during their holiday or beforehand despite Sarah's keen observation as a trained artist and psychic, which surely indicated how very cunning Kath could be. Furthermore, if Sarah arrived to find her persisting in the deception of identity more than two years on to hide herself from people like John Smith, she should expect Kath to be very dangerous indeed when cornered in confrontation. For her own safety Sarah would need to use the advantages of surprise and place to their greatest possible effect, to counter her adversary's desperation.

That made the where and when obvious: on home ground as soon as possible, before any possible local gossip had a chance to betray her. Down at the cottage beside the beach would be the best place, for though Kath would know the terrain Sarah knew it too, and the dunes would give cover for Smith and his men.

She would find out Kath's routine and go in without delay to ensure she did not risk losing the element of surprise.

What preparation work would she need to do beforehand, then, and how would she be able to do it? There was a possibility that Kath Brown already knew she had returned to the homeland and was expecting her visit: she might already have gone into cover. Sarah decided to ask her longstanding friend Shana Daily for help. Even if Shana would not receive her on the strength of their earlier friendship and her present importunity, she would receive her on army authority in this military state. Sarah would travel to Shana's farm and make the commune her base while she assessed the changes in the county and ascertained Kath Brown's true position. Then she would be able to make her final decisions regarding place and time and approach.

How could she entrap Kath Brown? With eloquent speeches; with facts; with strength or force; with tearful entreaties, or calls on her conscience? Sarah shook her head. The brash young woman she had known as Kath Brown clearly had no conscience and would not be swayed into confession by any of those devices. Events had proved that the apparent ruthlessness in her character was not the distortion of diffidence but a fact; and Kath had been the quiet sort who could take without self pity quite as much as she gave others. She seemed unassailable at first, but Sarah reminded herself that all people have their faults: she too would have hers. Sarah placed a mental image of Kath Brown beside the yardstick of Jesus Christ and saw at once from stance alone that her adversary lacked humility. Kath Brown could be brought down by the weakness of her pride. If God did not guide Sarah to try a different approach, that would be the weapon she would use against her.

Finally, once again Sarah asked herself why she was going to challenge Kath Brown to check that her motives were not suspect. She had to be sure that Kath deserved the outcome of the meeting and that the issues were not being distorted by any vindictiveness on her own part. Kath should be given an adequate chance to explain her actions and the reasons behind them to ensure that she got only the just deserts of her confessed deeds. That was far more than she had allowed Sarah if John Smith was to be believed.

Sarah drew her thoughts up sharply to hear such self pity, but found it more difficult than before to throw out her growing resentment against Kath Brown. By allowing herself the luxury of anticipating tomorrows she had also accidentally let in the unaffordable luxury of dwelling on unpleasant yesterdays; but there was only one day in which she could live, and that was today. She firmly placed tomorrow's business on the top shelf of her mind, yesterday's business in the dustbin, and concentrated on today's business of driving north.

Today had enough problems of its own. She had left the city hotel with a full fuel tank which would be just about enough to take her all the way straight home, but not enough to take a detour through the mountains to the west coast first. Not knowing whether she would be able to get petrol in her home county, she would need to refuel before she left the motorway, but that might involve explaining her change of route to an army unit and thereby giving John Smith a chance to veto her plan.

The little car passed the shire boundary and brought her at last back into her home county. She cheered, as she had always cheered to see that marker, and the county's traditional welcome of light rain when the rest of the country was fair; and she had been a longer time away before this homecoming than she had been before. Though at least two hours of driving still lay ahead, she already felt at home again and more secure. Whatever had happened in the past, and whatever hold John Smith might think he had over her, and whatever the state of the community she headed for, she was home at last and knew that unless she chose to go, this time no-one would be able to take her away.

And unexpectedly, raising new hopes, the car radio crackled into life.

CHAPTER 20

Sarah's heart raced as she tried to tune the radio in to the station while continuing to drive. She could hear the voices of two distant northern male broadcasters badly distorted by loud crackling and storm interference. Though their words were indecipherable, they were clearly transmitting to an audience they knew was there. The population of the county may have been decimated but a significant number had survived.

She turned off at the next service station to see whether she could pick up the radio broadcast more clearly while stationary. As she rounded a bend through some bushes screening the station from the carriageway, she almost ran over an army patrol monitoring the motorway from the cover of the hedgerow. The two men leapt out of the way and shouted affable rebukes after her car. She sounded her horn in reply and drove past their landrover into the car park.

The service area consisted of a drizzle-stained single storey building standing in a sloping plain of black tarmac. She parked outside the plate glass doors dividing the stone-faced part of the building from the glass-walled restaurant, and thought how little the place appeared to have changed except for the absence of vehicles in the car park and people in the foyer. The service area appeared deserted. Only a couple of army trucks and three landrovers parked in the H.G.V. area and a single light in the restaurant gave any suggestion of life at all.

The station had been a favourite stopping place for her during long journeys in the past. In the winter she used to check the weather reports for the mountain passes which could be treacherous and changeable. The station staff had always been pleasant and welcoming. It was saddening to think that they had probably gone.

Sarah shrugged off the memories and turned back to the radio. She knew she would learn far more from one half-hour current affairs programme than she had from three days' verbal fencing with John Smith. Disappointingly, the mountains still prevented her receiver from picking up the broadcast clearly enough for her to understand it. She gave up, hoping that the signal would improve once she had driven through the mountain range.

A young corporal left the station foyer and strolled across to her car. He had identified her by her vehicle as the woman his unit had received instructions to assist.

'Good afternoon, Ma'am. Need any help?' he asked.

She wound down her window with a grateful smile. In her alternative vision the young man appeared to be coping as best he could with continuing personal tragedy. She silently asked God to help him and then replied.

'Can you tell me, is it possible to get some petrol here?'

'No problem: round the other side of the building on your way out. Go in and get a bite to eat too if you're hungry.'

'Thanks, but I don't have the money.'

'You don't need any money here, Miss Brown. Have a good journey.'

He touched his peaked hat and strolled on to take a seat in one of the army trucks. She decided to take up his invitation, locked the car and went inside.

Dusk was starting to gather in, she noticed as she glanced back in the dimly lit foyer and saw the hint of twilight through the double barrier of the glass doors. She turned right and pushed through the internal swing doors into the cafeteria service restaurant.

The restaurant was still decorated in light beige and emerald green, just as she remembered it, but the refrigeration unit and the servery hotplates were bare, and all but one of the customer tables was unoccupied. The lonely figure seated at a table in the centre of the restaurant, was a portly woman whose back was turned to her as she sipped a cup of cold tea. Sarah could remember sitting there like that herself once in the past when she was waiting for better news about the road ahead after a snowstorm.

'What can I get you, Miss Brown?' asked a man from behind the food counter.

Sarah started in surprise and looked up to address the young man. He was a boyish-faced officer from the army catering corps, with a fresh expression and a friendly smile.

'I don't want to be any trouble,' she said.

'It's no trouble, I assure you. And you look like you could do with a good meal. What will you have? If you want to be quick I'll make you beans on toast, or if you've a bit more time to spare I can make you something really nice; say, chicken breast in supreme sauce?'

She smiled wryly.

'I've got beans time but not a beans appetite. I've eaten a lot of beans recently.'

'Haven't we all!' he laughed. 'How about a late breakfast, Miss Brown: bacon and eggs, fried bread, tomatoes, toast?'

'Sounds lovely. But please, stop calling me Miss Brown. I'm known as Katy.'

'And I'm Geoff. It's real nice to make your acquaintance, Katy.'

They shook hands over the servery unit. She tried not to show her dislike of the allied influence in the way he spoke. He felt pleased to find he naturally liked the person he had just been ordered to befriend.

'I expect you could do with some company too, Katy. Come round to the kitchens if you like. We can chat while I cook your food.'

She looked thoughtfully at him and gauged his invitation as being prompted by his natural friendliness. With a friendly smile in return, she walked round the counter and followed him through the kitchen doors.

The kitchens were a vision of gleaming stainless steel against beige ceramic tiles. She praised him for their cleanliness, but he shrugged off her compliment saying that it was just a part of his duties to keep the equipment clean. He opened one of the larder fridges and took out some rashers of bacon and two eggs. She saw the well-stocked shelves in surprise and commented as he began to prepare the food.

'It all seems so normal here,' she said, a slight catch in her voice.

'Normal? Of course it's normal. Why shouldn't it be?' he said offhandedly, concentrating more on his task than his reply.

'I don't know. I've just come up from the south. It's not normal there.'

'Has it ever been normal there?' he asked flippantly with a side smile.

'The south east is dead.'

Her grave tone drew him up with a reminder of others' suffering. He paused to place three rashers on the hotplate in front of him.

'I'm sorry, Katy: I forgot some people still get disturbed by it all. Then you should find this county a refreshing change. You get the other side of these mountains, you could be fooled into thinking nothing has happened at all.'

She looked incredulously at him. He nodded to affirm his statement.

'I couldn't believe it myself either at first. The war was gossip for a week, maybe, but the locals just carried on as normal. It's lucky for the rest of us they did, and others like them, some say. We could still feed ourselves and clothe ourselves. We could lick our wounds in private without having to invite the rest of the world to see our damage with a request for aid. Just as well, really, considering what's left of the world doesn't have much left to give.'

'I always suspected much of this county totally ignored central government except when it suited people not to. A sort of retaliation for being ignored economically, I used to think. It was always poor, but it made a good place to hide.'

'Is that why you're going back?'

'No. There's no place to hide now, is there. Where you're not, the allied forces are. I don't mind our own soldiers, but the rest unsettle me.'

'Don't worry: they'll be gone soon enough. As soon as the evidence is confirmed and they're implicated beyond doubt, they'll be getting their marching orders. There's few of us who don't feel like you these days.'

His words reminded Sarah of the conversation in the southern inn when Doug Chandler and Stephen had quipped with the barman about bleeding money out of the allied soldiers instead of taking their blood.

'I've heard it said that the allies may have been the ones to have started it,' she encouraged.

He nodded and cracked two eggs onto the hotplate.

'So you heard that down south too, eh? I thought it was just local talk. Some even claimed the allies gave the other side a fake tip about a pretend strike; only the other side believed it.'

'You mean, the other side found evidence to back up the tip off and struck back....'

Her voice trailed off as she realised she was probably saying too much at that stage and to that person. She could see her statement had made an impression on him. He realised she had given him some new insights into the barrack room gossip he had been airing for her benefit. His orders to befriend her now made sense.

'Do you think we will ever get enough evidence to confirm that?' he speculated.

She shrugged her shoulders.

'If I was the person who'd done a thing like that, the last place you'd find me three years later is still hanging around the country I'd betrayed.'

'True, Katy. But if you were a member of the government who had put those people up to that, would you welcome them home with honours? Would you welcome them home at all?'

She stared through him as she considered the implications of the point he had made. She had not asked herself before why Kath Brown had gone to such trouble to betray her country, and knew at once that the ideological mantle did not fit. The alternative struck her like a revelation: it made so much else fit into place that she struck the counter with excitement at working it out.

'Of course! An industrial spy: an information trader; and hollowed out books!' she cried: 'Of course I had to go along – I was the finishing touch.'

He looked up at her in concern.

'Are you all right?' he asked.

'Yes, Geoff: ignore me. I haven't been the same since the night of fires.'

Her unexpected defensiveness disappointed him. He tried to return their exchange to a conversational level.

'Why? What happened to you on Coronation Day?'

She stared at him in consternation, stunned by the obviousness of the solution to that riddle which she had been struggling to solve. She had realised at the midland city hotel that the new King had become the ruler, but had assumed incorrectly that the previous ruler had died with the subjects in the capital on the morning of the bombs. The night of fires had referred to the chain of hilltop beacons traditionally lit to notify the country of the accession of a new monarch.

'How many days was it after Coronation Day that the bombs struck?' she asked.

'Five,' he replied, surprised at her question: everybody else knew that.

She saw his surprise and hastily covered herself with a jocular excuse.

'That's what's wrong with me! One part of my life, I've got a memory like a sieve.'

He nodded sympathetically and began to plate her meal.

'You're not the only one, Katy: there's plenty with that problem now, and worse. Take that woman at the tables outside.' He nodded to the door into the restaurant and continued, 'Mrs McArthur. No-one knows where she's from; no-one knows much about her at all, least of all herself. All she does each day is sit at a table looking at a cup of tea, no milk, two sugars, and she talks to herself about the day the bombs fell. Come evening she picks up her bag and wanders off to a hovel of a cottage that used to be a byre. Just another of the casualties, one of the walking wounded, emotionally shot up. But I think maybe all of us are that.'

'You seem bright enough to me.'

'Maybe I learnt sooner than others how to shake it off. It's no good wishing yesterday didn't happen, 'cause it did, and we can't change that. And it's no good wishing for a brave new world 'cause there's no-one there to help us – there never is when you're bankrupt. So we may as well get on with what we've got: at least we won't get further into debt. Come on: I'll take this through for you.'

He placed her two plates of food on a tray and led the way back out into the restaurant. She followed thoughtfully, thinking through his talk of debt and bankruptcy to other considerations of finance relating to the information he had fed her. Had Kath Brown simply been selling a document or a service to the highest bidder? Had Sarah been betrayed not for ideals or ideologies, but for no more than thirty pieces of silver, the death price of a slave? She marvelled again with the bitterness of defeat at the way the devil had turned personal greed into national destruction without even being acknowledged as the initiator. How ignorant the wise had been to allow themselves to be deceived into such a fall.

CHAPTER 21

Sarah lost the radio station completely as she drove on into the mountains in the last light of evening. She impatiently turned the radio off and drove in silence, leaving the motorway to take the main road towards the passes through the heart of the mountain range. Behind the purple silhouette of the rugged horizon the sky deepened from its last puce pinks with lilac streamers into darkness. Immediately overhead reached the gaunt black outlines of hedgerow trees, their gnarled sturdy trunks standing out in the beams of her headlights.

It was in exactly that light that she had come that way the first time eight years ago with Shana Daly. They were travelling to Shana's farm where she spent the next four months on a working holiday, hay-timing and harvesting while she decided what she wanted to do next. At the time she had been naïve enough to think she had decided what to do with the rest of her life, still lacking that mature humility which knows life does not happen to order. She had returned to the capital after the holiday confident that she would be a success.

The success she envisaged did not come. The capital was an expensive place to live, the office routine to finance her life as an artist was drudgery to her, and she found herself outgrowing all her favourite haunts. She took stock, threw up everything and jumped on a train north to start a new life. In this beautiful county she discovered that nothing material could be so beautiful without also being hard. Life forced her to compromise in ways she would have scorned when a fierily idealistic student. She had moved on from that stage and had become a student of a different school. Seven years later, she could now see that she did have some success when considering life as a whole, for despite everything she was one of the survivors: in this changed world there was little more successful than that.

The main road snaked through the foothills, bypassing the grey slate town which had once been considered the gateway to the region. The broad wide road had once thronged with seasonal tourist traffic but was now deserted. Its condition was good, supporting Geoff's claim that life was carrying on as normal in this remote county.

The road emerged from a cutting and skirted a hillside overlooking a town in the valley below to her right, revealing a dark drop studded with twinkling lights. She gasped in amazement at the sight. Tears of joy sprung to her eyes, for the lights told her she was not alone, that homeland civilisation was still more than the army regime of necessity. The view tempted her to turn off and drive into the town but she resisted it. Her confrontation with Kath Brown compelled her to press on across the county rather than risk any chance of losing the element of surprise. If she achieved her objective at Dubmill, she would have more than enough time to visit this lovely market town again. She drove on along the undulating road through the foothills into the black mass of the mountains.

The road began to show slight touches of the blight which had scorched the rest of the country. A large roadside petrol station had closed and the café beside it had fallen into disrepair. A tourist information layby had gone and damaged road signs had not been replaced. The blight was not too severe though, for around another bend the windows of a roadside house blazed electric light onto a patch of pavement.

Ten minutes later her car rattled over a level crossing into the largest of the villages on her route. Lights shone from the windows of the houses, illuminating both sides of the street and the awkward stone bridge over the river at its heart. She choked up with joy to find a village so alive after spending a week passing through so many ghost towns. As her car left the village on the winding foothill road, she felt far more hopeful about what lay ahead.

The twisting road climbed higher, leading ever closer to the heart of the mountains. Then suddenly, unexpectedly as it had always seemed to her on that country road, she rounded yet another bend and discovered she had arrived at the first lake.

The twinkling lights of the lakeside town were reflected in the black waters of the lake. Formerly a popular place for tourists, all its large slate hotels and small stone houses still had bright lights in the windows and blazing fires in the hearths. On the pavement friendly people with smiling faces raised hands to wave at the stranger driving the unfamiliar car through their midst. She waved back and drove on past the busy ferry dock, taking the lakeside road back out of town into the country, heading north to travel west because of the mountains in between.

Along the next stretch of the main road former lakeside hotels showed less friendly faces, their welcome signs changed to factory names, their drives gated and secure. Beyond them the road looked progressively less well-maintained. Back in the darkness of the wild countryside, unexpected rock falls and fallen trees obstructed the poorly drained road in awkward places, forcing her to drive much more slowly.

She began to fear that the road might not be open all the way through the mountains. That would mean losing precious time doubling back to catch the ferry across the lake to try a different route. Quickly she countered the fear with the reassurance that whatever the outcome, it would all be just a part of God's will for her. All she needed to do was to drive on in the appropriate manner for the conditions and let God do the rest.

The strain of the journey began to tell on her. She started to wonder whether she was wise in trying to reach the commune that night. Shana Daly had always been an emotional woman and could be extremely demanding when her balance of mind was disturbed. In their last telephone conversation Shana had sounded like one of the walking wounded, the emotionally shot up as Geoff had so graphically described such instability, and

Sarah already felt too tired after a day of dodging potholes and rock falls to cope sympathetically with that. Or had Sarah got the wrong impression from that entirely unexpected telephone call when she had introduced herself as someone she was not, someone Shana had never liked.

The note of the working engine dropped as the car started to climb the pass through the heart of the mountains. She nursed the engine carefully, changing down the gears until she topped the summit and the car picked up speed again.

On the far side of the pass the road narrowed, hemmed in by tall encroaching dry-stone walls as it led down in to the savage glacial valley beyond. On either side grew a dark unnatural forest of evergreen, with a long ribbon of an island-studded lake through the spruce trees to the left, invisible in the darkness. The neglected road ran parallel to the lake on its east side. Pools of surface water stood where drains had become blocked with tree litter and not cleared. Dry-stone walls had collapsed in places, shedding boulders across the tarmac. Rock had fallen from the jagged faces blasted when the road had first been cut through and later widened.

The route demanded her full attention and all her driving skills to negotiate without mishap. At the end of the lake she thought too soon that she had made it safely through. A rock fall in a forgotten cutting had shed large boulders and loose debris over most of the road. She turned the corner to see the boulders standing out in her headlight beams and swerved to avoid them. Too close to miss the fall completely, she felt a thud as her front nearside tyre ran over a sharp slab of slate.

She knew at once that the tyre had been damaged, because the car was no longer responding well to the steering wheel. With the darkness of the wild countryside surrounding her, she knew she would not be able to check the tyre because she had no torch. She stopped the car and sat wondering what she should do.

CHAPTER 22

Sarah opened the car window to listen to the sounds of the wild country night. As she did not want to sleep in the car all night, her only course of action was to continue the journey. She started up the engine and gingerly drove on along the rubble-strewn road. Around the next bend the cutting dropped away to reveal an undulating valley. Distant lights shone across the valley through the darkness, lights that corresponded with the position of an old wayside inn she had visited in the past. Hoping the inn would still hold a welcome, she nursed the car down a gentle hill and along a winding mile in the valley bottom, concerned not to damage the wheel more than necessary in case she needed to reuse it later.

At length she reached the old inn and drew up outside the long white-walled building. The familiar black name board was still up above the door, spelling out 'The King's Head' in bold white letters. She locked up her car, thanking God for making the decision for her not to go on that night, and strolled inside.

The inn's welcome was just as it had been in the old days, the before the bomb days. In the warm slightly smoky atmosphere of the lounge bar a couple of prosperous looking farmers turned round from joking with the landlord at the counter, their ruddy faces shining in the gentle yellow light.

'Good evening, Ma'am. What can I get you?' the landlord asked, surprised to see a stranger.

She gave him an uncertain smile in the face of the farmers' curiosity about the arrival of someone they did not know, and nervously made her request.

'My car's broken down. I wondered if I could stay here the night and get it sorted in the morning?'

The landlord smiled warmly.

'Step right in and sit yourself at the fire.'

He called out for his wife to prepare a guest room for the first guest in two years, and to find a bite of supper for her. The phone number John Smith had given her in case of trouble sorted out the financial arrangements for her stay. It was answered by a man who called himself the editor of *Now!* Magazine and who quickly dealt with the landlord's queries, promising to repay him well for assisting top photographer Miss Katy Brown with her accommodation and the repairs to her car.

Sarah dined on a simple but satisfying meal of home-cooked tatie-pot and a steamed pudding. After eating, she sat back replete in a comfortable captain's chair by a blazing log fire in the inglenook fireplace, with a glass of ginger ale beside her on the table.

A lot of speculative whispering was going on at the bar about the presence of a reporter from *Now!* Magazine. One of the regular evening customers decided to try a personal approach to find out more. He crossed over to the inglenook, checked that she had no objection to him joining her, and sat down in the vacant chair opposite her beside the fire.

'You're not from these parts then, Miss Brown,' he opened directly in the local manner. She knew he must have got her name from the landlord but did not mind.

'No, I'm not, Mr, er...?'

'Tom Jennings,' he replied, and shook her hand with confident brevity.

He was a tall middle-aged man who did not look his height because of his girth. He wore heavy woollen trousers and a hand-knitted amber cardigan over a clean grey and white cotton shirt. His face was broad and amiable, framed with wavy auburn hair. The expression in his eyes was friendly but patronising. Here, Sarah thought, was a conceited man who would tell her a lot of biased information if she flattered his vanity. She encouraged him to chat by inviting him to speak with her on first-name terms.

'What brings a professional lady like you up to these parts then, Katy?' he asked.

'You know what the press are like, Tom: always after a good story. The way this county has survived, there has to be a good story here.'

He stretched expansively in his seat, pleased to find a well-spoken southerner such a willing audience for his opinions.

'Oh, aye,' he agreed: 'Aye, the capital thought it could do without us; but where are they now, I always say. Don't I, Stan.'

The landlord agreed distantly from behind the bar as he served up another round of drinks to the regulars who were listening intently to far more than their own incidental chat about lambing.

'Not that this county got off scot free, like,' Tom continued: 'But we kept going, just like we've always done in a crisis; and look at us now – leading the nation in organising elections to get a democratic government back in power. Aren't we, Stan.'

'You don't want to be listening to Tom, you know, Miss Brown,' the landlord warned her with a grin: 'He'll be telling you next he'll be seeing the King about it all in a week's time!'

'I am too!' Tom asserted to rebut the landlord's derision.

Sarah's ears pricked up.

'You mean you're going to the second meeting at the midland hotel too, Tom?' she asked quietly.

He faltered slightly, feeling wrong-footed.

'Ah, I didn't go to the first meeting. No fuel, didn't think it necessary with the other meeting on next week. You know how it is these days.'

She smiled to have placed him at a disadvantage so easily and knew God must have given her the right words because she had no natural talent for such tactics. Tom now thought her to be far more knowledgeable than she really was. She touched her khaki collar significantly and leaned across as though to whisper a confidence.

'This uniform, of course, is just a blind, Tom. We certainly don't print all we hear. This conversation, after all, is no more than a quiet off the record after dinner social chat.'

'Of course,' he agreed, his conspiratorial veneer too thin to hide his surprised suspicion.

'I understand, Tom, that you have yourself been playing quite an important part in this bid to restore national democracy and elect a new government.'

He considered her facial expression before he decided how to answer such a tactical statement, sensing that she might be playing tricks with him.

'I've done my bit,' he hedged.

He ventured into a cautious statement of the part he had played. Her encouraging comments prompted him to expand from his meek beginnings into a progressively more self-glorifying speech that then turned into a rallying call for the new democracy being established by people like him.

She listened with a fixed smile which hid her dismay. Though she was glad to hear that the army's ascendency would soon be over, she was disappointed to learn that the old corruptions were only going to be replaced by new ones. The lawyers' bar in the capital would be replaced with a provincial legal system based on promoted magistrates and solicitors: the old school tie network replaced by local secret preferment societies. The two-tier taxation system of rates and levies providing government funding, would become a single locally evaluated and administered taxation system. Strategically important industries and infrastructure would be handed over to local business people to run, except for failing ones like the road network which the army would be required to manage and improve. As a part of these extensive changes, Tom had already become the private owner of a nearby reservoir, and hoped for other acquisitions later too.

Though she did not like the solutions he was propounding, she recognised in them a genuine attempt to gather up the scattered strings of society in a bid to reunite and reorganise the devastated nation. After seeing her country in ruins, any reorganisation of it seemed better than none. At least in the developing democracy his system would create, the populace would be able to debate and protest against unpopular measures, however corrupt the leaders might be. The army was also powerful enough to prevent the new democracy from evolving into a dictatorship, by threatening to take back control in a coup d'état should the new politicians go too far.

She also sensed that Tom was not being deliberately corrupt. The last thing he would have done had he intended any self-preferment was to tell her the detail of his reforms so ingenuously. This was no confession by candlelight, but his rallying speech to persuade her to join the cause and help him rebuild the country. If his way was the only solution on offer, she knew that she probably would join his cause and help, while hoping that she would be able to change certain parts of the manifesto later through the new political machinery, to ensure that the new democratic government would give adequate representation for all.

She wondered whether all the new reforming politicians were like him. Would those who sought public office now be able to maintain that traditional veneer of public altruism over their proud self-interest, after such destruction? Did any genuine altruists still exist? She considered the few people she had met since her return to the homeland and identified all but one of them as either calculating or disenchanted people. The one altruist was the Minister, a religionist also, and he too was now dead. Then could non-religious idealism survive such social shock? And how would such speculation help her face Kath Brown? She dismissed her roaming thoughts and returned her full attention to what Tom Jennings had to say.

He was summing up his rallying speech with his vision of the future, a homely image intended to make the greatest impact on his hearers. It caught so accurately a feeling in her own heart that she felt pangs of yearning for his vision to be realised. He described a nation back at work again, providing for the common good through contributions to a common purse, and earning enough to be able to live well. He described homes for families and better care for the elderly and better education for the children and better medical care for the sick and better help for the disabled. He described a rebuilt country fit for heroes with a support system worthy of heroes and the children of heroes. He described the lights on again across the land, and joy and hope once more lighting the eyes of all the people.

She smiled sadly and shook her head. Though she wanted to believe him she knew, as the young army caterer had known, that such pipe dreams would never become anything more than smoke. She had heard it all before, had read the same dreams expressed after the previous world war. How quickly humanity could forget. And she, in the years to come; would she forget too?

CHAPTER 23

Sarah set off next morning far later than she had intended. She had slept in, having been able to relax naturally again among these ordinary people living their ordinary lives. While she had slept the landlord's son had replaced her damaged tyre with the spare tyre in the car boot and had checked over the car ready for her to continue her journey. She breakfasted well, heavy headed and slow in body, fielding off questions from the landlord's wife who wanted to know what story had really brought the young journalist there for her possibly not-so-by-chance overnight stop.

The day was overcast with a threat of rain as Sarah finally set out again. The chilly wind tossed the branches of the trees and turned over the leaves as if to herald a storm. Driving was easier in the daylight and the road north from the inn was in better condition than she had expected. She pressed on, keen to get to the commune and speak with Shana Daly before time ran out and Kath Brown was given another chance to escape.

Twenty minutes later her car emerged from the low pass out of the mountains and entered the outskirts of the nearby market town. The former tourist destination had now turned itself into an industrial and manufacturing centre. The hikers and mountaineers had gone. Now local residents thronged the shops and pavements. They turned to watch as the strange car passed between them through the narrow winding streets. Sarah drove on past them heading out of town to join the main road west.

She was less than an hour away from the commune at that point, if the roads held; and equally close to her cottage and Kath Brown if she but turned right instead of left at the next major road junction. Her heart quickened at the tempting thought of heading north and finding immediate resolution, but she quickly blocked it. Her conclusions from using the six serving men had highlighted the importance of finding out as much as possible about the situation at Dubmill before she went to challenge Kath.

She drove on past another lake turned reservoir and recalled Tom Jennings' master plan. There would be plenty of redundant reservoirs in the country now, she thought scornfully, but stopped mocking when she realised that if the nation made a rapid recovery those reservoirs could soon be back in demand again. Perhaps Tom Jennings was not so foolish to have awarded himself a lake, especially one with a lovely wooded island. Perhaps, once the running was all over, she daydreamed, she would also be able to negotiate an attractive lake with a wooded island for herself, instead of one of those detached common side houses in the southern suburbs of the capital.

At the end of the lake the road followed a river along the plain heading towards the coast. A few miles further on Sarah turned left onto a winding main road south west which linked some of the farming villages on the coastal plain and skirted the foothills of the mountain range. She turned left again onto a narrow lane which headed due south through several familiar farming hamlets back towards the mountains. At a small village lying in the shadow of the westernmost ridge of the mountain range, she turned left once more by a little stone bridge over a tree-shaded river. A few yards further on she drew up her car and parked at the road gate barring the track to Fairfield Farm.

Sarah got out of her car and leaned against the top bar of the wooden gate to gaze at the view across the fields and the mountains beyond. She savoured the achievement of standing there looking at that view again, despite all that had happened since her phone call from the capital, and everything else that had happened in the last three years. After a lifetime of apparent failure, she had succeeded in a real challenge at last. Her success gave her new confidence in herself and new courage to face the world.

Beyond the fence of barbed wire strands, the roadside field was being grazed by lambing ewes. On the far side a gaunt figure gazed dispiritedly at a small weak newborn lamb. Sarah recognised Shana at once and vaulted the five-bar gate to run down the track towards her, calling her name.

Shana sprung round in surprise. At once her joyless face lit up with a radiant smile of welcome.

'Sarah!' she cried out.

The two friends ran to greet each other and embraced in joy over the barbed wire fence.

'What a surprise, Sarah! We thought you were dead!' Shana exclaimed. She looked askance at Sarah's clothes. 'What's with the army fatigues?'

'It's a long story,' Sarah said. She looked Shana up and down, concerned to see how unwell her friend appeared.

Shana was dressed in a collection of tattered old jumpers and a pair of well-patched dungarees tucked into her rubber boots. Her long honey-blonde hair was pinned up in a windblown bun, and stray locks fluttered across her gaunt, pallid face.

'I'm so glad you're alive, Shana,' Sarah said. 'I have so much to tell you, and there's so much news I want to hear. But first I must ask you to call me Katy, if you're still prepared to invite me inside after that awful phone call I made to you from Tony's.'

'So it was you ringing from the capital last week! I was sure it was, but Paul said no. He thought my....'

She turned aside to hide her embarrassment from her friend and finished her sentence addressing the sheep.

'... he thought my mind was playing tricks on me again.'

Sarah hugged Shana again in compassion, not offended that her friend had turned her back on her to hide her shame. She could identify with the turmoil she felt in Shana's mind, and prayed that she could pass on the blessing of God's healing to her friend as the Minister had done for her, by being the conduit for God to make Shana whole at last.

'I see you have a good number of lambs this year,' she said, looking across the field. The lamb Shana had been tending had managed to stand up on its wobbly legs and latch onto its mother's teat. Its tail began to shake with pleasure as it suckled its first taste of milk.

Shana kicked at a small stone in the grass, her hand in her pockets, linking the lambs with her own recently confirmed pregnancy.

'These sheep? Their lambs are half the size they should be. Everything we breed or grow now is stunted and underweight. The politicians have a lot to answer for; the people who put our country in the way of the bombs and ruined our land in the withering wind.'

Shana's bitterness tugged at Sarah's own indignation. She hastily shut out the negative emotions and radiated back the love of God for all creatures.

'Perhaps they do, but who are we to judge,' Sarah said. 'We should rather be taking care of all the good things God has chosen to give us today. Maybe these lambs are stunted; but they are new: they were born after the night of fires. These little lives are symbols of far more significance than the damage to stock – they are the heralds of rebirth.'

Shana stared at her in disbelief and tossed her head in scorn.

'You mention God? After all that has happened you dare to suggest I should thank God? No! No, no: you come with me to the house, and I'll show you your God!'

Shana pressed Sarah to drive to the farmstead and instructed her to park her car out of sight in one of the barns. As they crossed the yard to the two-hundred-year-old stone farmhouse, Shana continued.

'Where was God when all those children died? Where was God when all the refugees got burnt? Where was God when all the cities were wiped out?'

Sarah replied with gentle power, 'God was comforting the

children, grieving for them, taking them home to heaven. God was walking with the refugees, giving them the courage to face their hardships, saddened by the injustice of their fate, knowing what it felt like because God as Jesus had also been a refugee. God was there in the cities and in the country, seeing God's beautiful creation destroyed by the withering winds, angered by the loss of so much that was innocent and wonderfully made, so much good destroyed by fear and hatred.'

Shana opened the back door into the dim welcome of the farmhouse kitchen. The aroma of stewing meat issued mouth-wateringly from the solid fuel stove that had taken the place of an earlier old range. Sarah sat down at the scrubbed pine table, appreciating once again the peaceful simplicity of the room.

'No, that's not God. I'll show you the real God!' Shana cried, and left the room to fetch a Bible.

Sarah knew from past experience that when Shana railed against the powers controlling life, her defiance was a smokescreen hiding her dissatisfaction with herself. Sarah needed to break through that screen to help her. She took care not to be offended when Shana threw a Bible down in front of her. The book was open at the twenty-sixth chapter of Leviticus.

'There! Is that the statement of an ever-loving God?' Shana demanded.

She left Sarah to read the chapter while she made a pot of tea, but interrupted her reading while she waited for the tea to brew.

'Don't tell me it's fair when God says the sins of the fathers shall be visited on the sons!'

Sarah looked up from the Bible with compassionate forbearance.

'That wasn't an unjust new decree of God's, Shana – that's just a fact of life. Weren't our fathers the politicians who permitted us to live in the shadow of the bombs, and aren't we and our children the people who live with the consequences of their decisions, now that events have proved those decisions wrong?'

'Come on! Look at what's written there!' Shana exclaimed, pointing at the middle of the chapter, apparently not having listened to Sarah's reply at all.

Sarah read on as Shana poured out the tea. In the passage she had pointed out the Lord told Moses what would happen to those who did not obey the Lord's commandments. In that particular translation several parts of the vivid description corresponded uncannily with what had happened to the nation since the night of fires. Sarah waited for Shana to sit down beside her with the tea before she gave her own interpretation of that passage.

'Long ago, around the dawn of history, God gave the world a set of simple laws and promises through Moses and the Israelites which became known as the old covenant, and this chapter is a part of that set. The principle of leaving fields fallow regularly is one of those laws which you will still be following here. These basic laws helped people live in community with each other. Not all the whys were explained but the orders were given, just like we do with young children.

'Then humanity moved up into the next class and people were given more individual responsibility with the new covenant. Instead of all the laws in the Old Testament we were given just two: to love God with all our hearts, minds, bodies and souls; and to love everyone else as ourselves. The new laws didn't replace the old laws but rather transcended them. How can I love my neighbour if my farming policy exhausts the land so that it's no longer capable of providing food for us both and turns into a desert?'

'But don't you see? Your argument is supporting my case, not disproving it.'

'Think on, Shana. What happens to a child who hasn't learnt its lessons at school? It's kept down in the same year and the same class until it does learn the lesson.'

'What, you mean we're no more civilised than people were

in twelve hundred B.C.E.?'

'Before the night of fires, yes. Society was degenerating fast, the way it always does when money becomes god and suppliers have to cater for the lowest common denominator. Our nation threw away its right to be judged under the new covenant by the way we couldn't even follow the most basic parts of the old, and that was our own fault as well as our leaders'. Even the church threw away its right to live and die by the new covenant – instead of living by faith in Jesus it made a god of the business model of management and enmeshed itself in rules and regulations little different from all that Jesus had tried to sweep away. Some individual church members tried to live the way of faith; but the rest of us were too busy eating fish on Friday and lamb at Easter to think of Jesus making us fishers of men and of Jesus being the lamb sacrificed for our iniquity at the world's Passover.

'No, we no longer needed to leave the land fallow when our agrichemicals could feed the dust-bowl fields and poison the wild creatures and ourselves. No, we no longer needed the Sabbath as a day of rest – after all, science had disproved God, hadn't it. There was no longer any need for all that socialist stuff about loving your neighbour and giving your spare coat to the poor: greed was good and we had become rich enough not to need other people except as customers. Need I go on? The taximeter still clocked up the cost whether we were in the cab or not. And I was no better than the rest - in my privileged position as a daughter of this nation....'

She broke off, realising that Shana was silently weeping. Shana took up the conversation, speaking in a low bitter voice from her own experience.

'... I let it cushion me from the realities of the world. I hid from the problem here, burying my head in the organic manure. I did understand what you lot were saying – we tried to live by it here on the farm, salving the national conscience. Less of the scientific wonder breakthroughs, a little more of the love and the labour intensive and the elbow grease. Not that science and religion are incompatible, I said: science is just the investigation of all the wonders God creates, I said. But I said it here, hiding in my little refuge, when I should have been out there pleading with the government of the day.'

Shana sipped her tea and then continued, 'If only I had spoken out about what I knew then. A creature will never be broken in to live the gentle way without the discipline of training; and without the discipline of respect no trained creature will continue to conform to the gentle way. The cycle of life, growth and death should be a part of that discipline of the gentle way. But the way we raped and pillaged the Earth our mother was not. We destroyed the planet for our children because of profits and the accumulation of wealth. And we may even have destroyed our children too, simply because I didn't stand up to be counted or persuade others to be counted too!'

Sarah touched Shana's right forearm on the tabletop, recognising from her own past how her friend was being deceived by the devil into believing herself solely responsible for the collective conscience of the nation and therefore for its fall.

'Oh, Shana, we did what we thought was right at the time. We tried our best – why you even lived it. What more could you or I have possibly done or said that hadn't already been done or said by the environmentalists, the women's peace movement, the disarmament groups, the orthodox church and other sects, denominations and religions, even some of the politicians and landowners and trade unionists. And for some reason we two have been included in the number that survived. That was God's choice for us, even though there were many far more worthy than us of being saved who died. Here in this chapter of Leviticus God tells us what to do now: to humble ourselves, to confess our faults, to make amends for our errors, and then to get on with living.

'What is the use of feeling guilt and remorse because of our past mistakes if we just wallow in self pity instead of learning from them and building on a better foundation? Hell has many forms, all with one common feature: separation from God, and self-pity is one of those. But heaven can be found in the strangest of places, and the kingdom of heaven is wherever God is. Heaven and hell both exist here right now. It is your choice which one you live in at any time. And if you want to know the appropriate steps to take in either direction, this book will tell you the way.'

Sarah pushed the open Bible across the table to her friend. Shana picked up the book to look again at the text, but snapped it shut nervously on hearing footsteps at the back door. Her husband Paul came in with two of the communers Ted and Roger, discussing some fence repairs they had just finished. Shana put her old false smile back on her face and introduced Katy Brown to her household. Introductions over, they finished setting the table in preparation for lunch. Sarah watched Shana thoughtfully as they worked, wondering whether her words had had any effect at all.

CHAPTER 24

After supper each evening, the communers liked to relax together around the fire in the lounge of the main house and watch the evening news on local television. Sarah sat with the others that evening and watched with concern to see how self-contained and self-confident the county had become. Afterwards they discussed an item of news and some of the incidents on the farm during the day, including Katy's arrival. By ten o'clock the communers took their leave and returned to their cottages and bothie rooms for the night. Shana left the lounge after them to heat some milk for bedtime drinks for those who were left. Sarah found herself alone with Paul in the lounge.

Paul was a fit, agile man in the prime of life, tall with a broad muscular frame which belied his height. He carried himself with an indolent manner, and his handsome fair-complexioned face had a perpetual half-smile ranging from enquiry to faint contempt. His expression often made it hard to perceive his sincerity; but Sarah sensed he was being sincere when he began to speak to her once they were alone.

'Katy Brown, as you call yourself now, I'm glad you've turned up here. I don't know what you said to my wife today, but she's getting better already.'

Sarah moved her gaze from the heart of the fire to stare through his expression as he lay draped across the chintz-covered armchair by the black-leaded fireplace.

'You mock me, Paul, just as you always used to,' she replied gently.

He nodded, understanding her caution about her name. Since the bombs dropped other friends of his had had name changes too to escape reputations earned before the night of fires. He had recognised Sarah at once and with introductions had immediately understood her problem even though she had told him nothing. By nature a practical man, he was willing to help her because of the way she had already helped his wife, in the hope that she would stay and continue to help them both.

'I don't mock intentionally, my little artist. You have only been here since lunchtime, I know; but I know my wife. Shana has been very sick, far worse than you ever saw her before, and your phone call from the capital did little indeed to help. And she is pregnant now so we cannot give her the medication, and we have no psychiatrist in the area anymore. I tried to contact you at home without success. Now I know why. At the time I could only presume that you were dead.'

'You mean, you found Kath Brown masquerading as Sarah Baylis, and now Sarah Baylis turning up as Katy Brown?'

'Even here you are not safe, Katy, at least not safe enough to talk about it openly. We haven't found out yet how or why, just that that is the case. That's what makes Shana's recovery so much harder this time – there is justification for some of her apparently irrational thoughts. But she is better today, I know; and it's not just that you're here. That tune she was humming as she prepared supper; her eyes clear of that strained look; her voice more melodic again. Whatever you said to her today has put her back on the right track. I'm very grateful. I want you to stay.'

Sarah tried to refuse him but he brushed her explanations aside.

'No, you must stay now: you can't leave at this point. I love Shana so much, but I don't know how to cope with her like this. All too easily I could destroy the good you've done, as I've managed so many times before when she's just starting to get better. I'd help you every way I could if you'd agree to stay and help her through.'

'Paul, you don't need to promise me anything to help Shana get better. She is my friend – I'd help her anyway. It's just that I have some unfinished business which I must complete first before I can promise anything, and this khaki I'm wearing shows the sort of people I'm behoven to. First, I have to see a woman about a dog called Bubbles Kamir.'

The smile broadened across Paul's face as he connected her allusion to the problem he realised she had to solve. If all it needed for her to say yes was his help in this, he would give it. Continuing her allusion for the sake of discretion, he informed her of some facts she would find useful to know.

'Yes, Sarah Baylis does still have a lurcher called Bubbles Kamir, and she does still live in that little beach cottage. She's come up in the world since you knew her as a kennel maid, with the kennels turning into an animal refuge centre. She seems to be so busy she doesn't paint any more, more's the pity. We have one of her better early works in our bedroom: *Swallows and Hawks*. Remember it?'

'She went as far as selling my work?' Sarah demanded indignantly.

'I think she was putting the old days behind her. She doesn't go to church anymore either. Funny how that holiday changed her.'

His tone of voice told her that he understood her position, but she checked his expression before she felt confident he really meant his offer of help. In her alternative vision he was like a mirror image of himself, but Shana was in that image too. She realised that she could trust him because he believed she held his wife's sanity in her hands.

'Paul, I need to pay a surprise call on that little madam at Dubmill. Yes, I will help you, if you can help me in that.'

He smiled fatuously, and taunted, 'So the army will allow it now.'

A doubt flashed through her mind. She threw it out, knowing he liked to play people to prove his superiority to himself by controlling others' fear. He often coaxed people to trust him and then made himself appear likely to betray that trust, but he had never been caught out in betrayal before. His mental games made Shana's recurring sickness no surprise, Sarah thought, and knew that if he did not change his ways, he could well suffer a swift fall. Men like John Smith would not tolerate his vagaries of character in the new homeland. She caught her breath to discover how she had begun to regard John Smith, and wondered whether her new respect for him was born of a more basic emotion than faith.

'I'm sorry, Katy: that was unfair of me,' Paul apologised perfunctorily on seeing her expression. 'May I suggest we pay your surprise call shortly after first light tomorrow, to make sure the bird has no chance of flying off forewarned? I believe her employer keeps her routine very similar to your own.'

'You seem to know a great deal about her, Paul.'

'I asked her to help Shana several times, but she wouldn't come. So in the end I took Shana over to her cottage to see her. It was embarrassing. Shana insisted she wasn't Sarah. I must admit I wasn't certain myself; nor was Neil, the chap who runs the refuge; but everything else fitted, and her papers were all right. So I just told Shana what Neil told me, that an awful lot must have been beaten out of her when she was arrested for smuggling Bibles on that holiday tour. After all, could I believe that I was going mad too? She wore your type of clothes, her hair was your sort of style, she spoke with your sort of accent and inflection. What if her voice was just a little higher? What if her face was sort of different with the make-up? I know you never used to wear make-up, but maybe after the holiday tour and everything that had happened you had changed.'

'What did happen after Sarah Baylis was arrested for smuggling Bibles?'

He looked thoughtfully at her, taken aback to think that she might not know that answer because she may have been more wrongfully engaged during the last three years than he had appreciated. He tested her with a question significantly emphasised to warn her of his concern.

'Don't you know, Katy?'

She blushed and hung her head in the face of his suspicion.
'Six months are missing out of my life, Paul, from the day
Sarah Baylis was arrested to the morning I woke up in a prison
cell on the other side with a chunk missing out of my mind, a
chunk missing out of my life, and no name, only the number
1376259. That's when I really started to understand Shana,
because that's when I started my own walks beyond sanity.'

While Sarah was still speaking Shana came back into the
lounge with the tray of bedtime drinks. She had overheard
Sarah's last sentence and looked across at Paul with fearful eyes
as she offered the tray to Sarah who took a mug of hot milk.

'Shana, what did Sarah tell you had happened to her on the
other side after she had been arrested for smuggling Bibles?'
Paul asked.

She did not answer immediately but played for time
handing Paul his mug of cocoa so that she could think out an
answer. After she had settled down on the sofa with a malted
drink she replied, nervously at first, but gaining confidence as
she spoke on.

'That Sarah didn't tell me all that much. The bus and all the
luggage were impounded, and everyone was questioned. Sarah
Baylis and Katherine Brown were both arrested for smuggling
Bibles in and for taking photos of sensitive installations. After
the arrests Sarah never saw Katherine again. Sarah was tried and
convicted of smuggling and began to serve a five-year sentence.
After representations by our embassy, Sarah made a formal
apology to the court and was deported. During her imprisonment
she was subjected to a regime which included a formal course of
dissuasion from her extreme religious beliefs.'

'And her friend?' Sarah asked, dry-mouthed.

'Sarah asked after Katherine at our embassy. The attaché
could tell her only that Katherine Brown had been tried and
convicted of espionage. Though the embassy was making all the
representations it could, she was led not to expect to see her
friend again.'

Sarah sat in silence, staring at her milk as she tried to come to terms with what she had just been told. Though she had already deduced Kath Brown's duplicity, it was still a great shock to have her deduction confirmed by someone else; as though Sarah had not really wanted to believe the truth of her travelling friend's callous betrayal of her trust.

'I didn't take those photographs,' she said, her voice barely audible, her expression betraying her emotions and her fear of being doubted by Paul and Shana at that late stage.

'Don't worry, little artist,' Paul reassured: 'We know who you are, and now you've turned up here we have all the proof we needed. We'll help you challenge her tomorrow, and if that doesn't work; well, you're staying here anyway – we'll help you find some other way that does work. You can stop running now, girl – you're amongst friends here.'

'So you are going to stay?' Shana asked, her eyes wide and shining.

Sarah nodded, her eyes glistening with gratitude to rediscover such loyal friendship after she had thought herself alone in the world. Never before had she understood so clearly how important a sense of belonging and a sense of past could be.

'If I can adopt you as my new family: all my family is dead,' she bartered.

'Done!' Paul agreed instantly, laughing, leaping up to shake her hand on the deal.

'As long as you don't mind adopting my Great Aunt Jenner as well,' Shana teased: 'She's one of those people, it doesn't matter what happens – fire, flood, earthquake, bombs, volcano – she comes out spotless with an urnful of tea and a first aid box; and an equally never-ending repertoire of starchy comments about what you should be doing too.'

'Yes, Shana, I'll even humour my new Great Auntie Jenner. Everyone should have one of those. They don't die – God just takes them home.'

Later that night, as Sarah waited for sleep to steal over her, she said a prayer of deep gratitude for the commune's welcome, for the friend's spare bed in which she lay, and for the warm sense of family homecoming she had felt that day for the first time in her life. At last God seemed to be making things come right for her, she thought, forgetting how things had had to come right in her own mind first for her to appreciate all that she had had before but had never noticed.

CHAPTER 25

They set off from the commune at first light in two landrovers. Sarah and Paul were in the first vehicle; Ted and Roger drove behind with three dogs. Sarah was wearing the blue work clothes she had liberated from the capital less than two weeks before, choosing to dress in the style of her new family in a conscious rejection of the army khaki.

As Sarah climbed into the passenger seat Paul put two shotguns in the back.

'But Paul, shooting her won't help,' she objected.

He shook Sarah off impatiently.

'This country's a different place now, lady. It's either you or her, and you're the friend she left to die.'

He climbed aboard and strapped himself into the driver's seat.

'Anyhow, we've been under watch again through the night. Probably your friend John Smith and his team, but maybe not. You can't be too careful these days, or too choosy.'

He started up the landrover, waved to the vehicle behind and drove off out of the yard. Sarah watched him closely in the reflected glow of the headlights and became aware of her physical arousal at his manliness. She quickly pushed away any thoughts of sexual attraction knowing that the person, the time and the place were all wrong. Then she realised her body had responded to his masculine strength because it was being exerted for her protection, not used against her as had so often been the case with men she had met in the recent past.

The rough cinder farm track stretched before them in the headlight beams as two pale ruts separated by a dark strip of long grass. On her side ran the barbed wire fence with the field of lambing ewes in the darkness beyond; on his side stood the gaunt hawthorn hedgerow topping the old dyke. The landrovers stopped at the road gate. She jumped out to let them through. As she closed the gate again after them the three sheepdogs set to barking. Alarmed, she ran back to Paul's landrover and climbed back inside. She saw at once what the problem was.

John Smith was standing at the open driver's door, his revolver aimed at Paul who had frozen with his left hand reaching back for one of the shotguns. A ring of armed soldiers stood ready to fire in case the two landrovers tried to bolt from the Fairfield track end, and the road was blocked by a canvas-walled army truck and a small black car. The landrovers were going nowhere.

'Our way, Miss Katy Brown; not your way,' Smith ordered forcefully.

'We are only trying to help our friend,' Paul said.

'But which one *is* your friend?' Smith challenged.

He barked out two orders to his men without taking his attention off the two people in the landrover. Paul's eyes glinted angrily at the way he had been stopped, but he knew from the troops surrounding him that he was helpless to escape the ambush and John Smith's command.

'Katy, you will go there with me,' Smith ordered. 'And the rest of you, as you are so keen to help, you can take some of my men over to the animal refuge in your jeeps, to make sure no-one else interferes. Come on, Katy! Move yourself: out you get!'

She obeyed, shaking as she jumped down, fearful of what Smith might do to Paul when she was out of range. No gunshot rang out, to her relief: instead two soldiers pushed their way aboard and Smith slammed shut the driver's door. Three more soldiers climbed in with Ted and Roger and the dogs. The other six bundled back into the army truck.

Smith hustled Sarah over to his little black car. As he checked she was safely strapped in to the passenger seat, she recalcitrantly recalled Tom Jennings' assurance that the army's ascendency would soon end, and wished that it already had. Smith started up the car and asked her for directions. She answered gruffly. He drove off at the head of the convoy along the country roads towards the coast. Sarah's fear began to turn to indignation at his intrusion. After they had left the farming village behind she found the courage to object.

'Why aren't you letting me do this my own way?'

'We are. Shotguns weren't your idea; and we want her taken alive. People like Paul Daly have learnt over the last two years to shoot first and ask questions later. That style of civilian justice has to come to an end now. The emergency months are over. It's time for the farmers to go back to shooting crows.'

The convoy crossed a hump-backed bridge and drove up into the next village. Passers-by on their way to work for first shift stepped back into doorways as the convoy passed. They had seen such convoys before with the black car at the head and the army truck at the rear escorting local people in the vehicles between. Their expressions and attitudes showed Sarah what the locals understood by such an incident.

'You are ruining Paul's reputation, John,' she said: 'The west coast is a close community. Those people outside all know him, and they can all see him being taken away.'

'Assisting the army, you mean,' Smith corrected.

He realised that she was still far too insubordinate for him to have any confidence in the outcome of the dawn raid, and decided to try to bring her more into line.

'Oh, woman, why do you insist on making such a fuss? These things don't matter at all. Yet you seem completely unmoved when everything is falling to pieces around you.'

She turned to look at him in the half light, her alternative vision picking up quite a different message from the exasperation he was trying to convey. She consciously began to observe his manly qualities for the first time, and found that when she stopped thinking of him as a dangerous army officer she was able to see his many good points.

'Perhaps instinctively I want to impress you,' she said.

He laughed. Though his laugh was derisive, she found it quite attractive. She wondered whether she would find his manliness as exciting as Paul's if used to assist her, and realised that she would prefer him because his character was more sound than Paul's. At least John Smith played with people's trust for more legitimate reasons than merely to boost his own ego.

'I expect you'll be glad when all this is over and you can get back to your family, John,' she said.

He laughed again, more derisively to block any unwanted attention.

'The army is my family, Katy Brown. That's all I want; and all I'll ever need.'

'What, you don't mind being all alone in the world?'

'In my line of work alone's the only way to be.'

They had reached the outskirts of the first coastal harbour town on their route. He turned right onto the main road following her directions, and led the convoy north along the coast.

'Woman, don't choose to set your cap at me. You wouldn't like what you get!' he warned. 'When all this is over, go find some Ted or Roger or Tom or Geoff, someone who can share your beliefs and your dreams. Now is the time to start building castles and founding empires. Don't miss out by jumping too soon – there are plenty of men now who would be very pleased to end up with a woman like you.'

'Where? Hiding in the ditches?' she scoffed in chagrin on having her device so effortlessly destroyed and thrown back at her.

'Don't be silly!' he scolded. 'If you have the faith in your God to save you from death and injustice, surely you can find the faith in your God to provide you with the good things you want in life too.'

She blushed to have her faith thrown back at her too so ably by such a non-believer. He heard the discomfort in her voice as she apologised to him for her outburst.

'I'm sorry. I misread your signs and was too proud to admit my mistake,' she said. 'You are right, of course. I was caught up in the feeling that time is running out. I was frightened I might miss my last chance.'

He sensed that behind this unexpectedly absurd conversation she was subconsciously frightened she would be the loser in the meeting ahead. To take her mind off the outcome, he tried to raise her indignation at him and her adversary instead.

'Lady, time hasn't yet run out for you, because you are still here!' he growled: 'It has run out for all those piles of dust in the cities. It's run out for your mother and your father and your grandparents and your great-grandparents; and it's run out for the politicians and the captains of industry and the kings and queens you learned about in school; and it runs out for maybe a hundred thousand or a million every week; but unless you're lying, time isn't running out yet for you. Time is only running out for Katherine Brown the photographer who somehow had a part in convincing the other side that the allied forces were going to drop nuclear bombs on them from our dear homeland, and who was therefore partly responsible for persuading the other side to pre-empt the fictitious strike using their secretly developed neutron bombs which are by far the nastiest nuclear bombs of all.'

'But how could Kath Brown do that?' Sarah scoffed.

'That is what we are all going to Dubmill beach cottage to find out.'

They drove on in silence except for the occasional exchange of directions along the coast road north. He began to fear he had been too harsh with her and had undermined her confidence. Her silence rather marked his success in arousing her resentment for Kath Brown which she was struggling to master, for she knew that while she acted in resentment, she could expect no strengthening help from God. She reminded herself that only by

God's grace had she found faith and been saved from a life like Kath's, that however large or small the offence they had both sinned and fallen short of the glory of God, that Kath must have been sick to have carried out such a plot. These arguments failed her. Troubled, she pleaded silently with God to take her resentment away, and prayed for the salvation of the woman she resented. At last her resentment began to lift. She was able to face the meeting in faith once more and to hand its outcome to the will of God.

'I'm sorry if I upset you just now,' Smith apologised genuinely.

'Don't be. It was necessary for me to face my resentment for Kath Brown and to overcome it before I meet her, not while we talk. Otherwise I might have said wrong things and done wrong things and completely spoilt everything. Now I am at peace again and God is in control.'

She guided him through the outskirts of the last coastal town on their route, and on left at the sharp bend after the church beyond, only a few miles from her home. He could feel the tension rising in himself but sensed none in her. Even though she knew her life hung in the balance at that one meeting and her fate would be decided before noon, she was facing the momentous occasion with complete equanimity and seemed to radiate an astonishing sense of calm.

'You know, I admire your faith, whatever it may be in,' he said reflectively. 'I lost my faith when my brother died. Gangrene is a nasty way to go, and we were very close. He had no heaven to go to and died screaming. But you face even death with dignity, and I know the sorts of hell you've already been through. Misguided faith, perhaps; but in a way I still envy you that.'

The ensuing silence was charged with his awkwardness at having made such an admission. She spoke to break the silence for him.

'Do you still blame Kath Brown for your brother's death?'

she asked softly.

Her question told him how misguided his hunger for vengeance had been, in a gentle way which her criticism could never have achieved.

'I also respect you, for not trying to persuade me to your way of thinking,' he said after a pause. 'You were confident your example alone would convert me. Your faith is no weakness to you, but your strength.'

Sarah sighed as her alternative vision took her back to the image of him she had seen during their breakfast in the haunted city hotel, the dashing young army officer with the peaked cap and the air of tragedy beneath his youthful spirits, like one who had recently survived a battle in which he had watched his best friend die. He too had emotions to bring into control that morning before her meeting with Kath Brown, to ensure that he did not continue to act through emotion rather than self control.

'Oh, I used to convert people, with a capital C,' she admitted brightly. 'Then I spent three years being persuaded that I was wrong – conversion in the opposite direction. That's taught me persuasion either way is wrong: words can be cheap; only personal example really convinces. No-one likes being told the way to go until they want to know for themselves and choose to ask. The signpost can say nothing to them until then, beyond the fact that it is there.'

They came to a physical signpost and Smith turned left onto a beach track, without her having to telling him to turn there. The rest of the convoy continued along the road they had turned off.

'You knew all along the way we were going?' she asked in surprise.

'Of course. I wouldn't take any risks at this late stage,' he said.

The mask had slipped back over his mind again, she sensed: he had turned himself back into the emotionless machine that his training enabled him to be. She left the man to hide behind the mask and asked the soldier where the convoy had gone.

He would not say even at that late stage for fear of spoiling the surprise and simply assured her that the rest of the team would take up adequate positions to ensure her safety. He parked his car in a position to block access to Dubmill Cottage along the beach track from the south. The army truck took up a similar position to block the beach road from the north, and the men fanned out through the dunes to take up armed vantage points along the beach. The two landrovers went straight to Dubmill Farm, home of the proprietor of the former kennels turned animal refuge. Neil Davison and his family woke up to find three soldiers and three civilians storming into his house while two more soldiers stood on guard outside. When Neil heard their explanation he was no longer surprised and offered them breakfast. He had been the first person to bring to the army's attention the changes he was noticing in his promoted kennel maid Sarah Baylis, and that had been some time before.

By dawn the beach cottage was surrounded and the trap had been set. Sarah had been equipped with a hidden miniature recorder transmitter and was lying beside Smith in the dunes overlooking the cottage, downwind to avoid alerting the dogs housed in the kennels screened by a clump of trees beyond.

The sun rose clear of the horizon, a bright white sun in a cloudless azure sky edged by the deep purple of the nearby mountains to the east and the indigo hills of the northern kingdom across the water to the northwest. The reassuring roll and retreat of the receding waves along the beach gave a background for the chorus of birdsong greeting the promising fresh new day from the hedgerows and the dunes and the thickets of trees. Animals began to move about more in the fields: some sheep and cattle, a goat, a string of horses brought there to the refuge while their previous owners were traced and their futures decided.

Down between the dunes and the edge of the beach stood the single storey wood and brick cottage which Sarah had found and restored herself seven years before. It was a humble home, hard to heat in the winter but a glorious place to live in the summer with those occasional days of endless sunshine and those brief nights of enchantment beneath the glittering stars.

The bedroom light came on in the cottage. Sarah clutched Smith's arm in excitement to find their quarry at home and looked into his face to see whether she should go. He shook his head and nodded down to the cottage to indicate to her to continue to watch.

Lights came on and went off around the cottage. She watched the impostor's movements around her house with disdain. Soon all the lights were switched off and a lone figure stepped outside. Despite the distance and the deceptive morning light, the figure was clearly not a youth or a small man but a woman clad in trousers and a jacket. She walked along the path to the kennels in the screen of trees. Her arrival was greeted by loud barking from a pack of assorted dogs. The barking quickly died down.

Again Sarah looked to Smith to see whether she should go to challenge the young woman who had taken her place. Again he shook his head, still not certain what support the woman they watched might have hidden in those buildings.

Some fifteen minutes later the woman emerged again from the kennels in the trees and took the path to the beach as she began exercising some of the dogs in her care. With her came two Alsatians pulling her along on leads, and an assortment of three she could trust to run loose which Sarah recognised at once.

Anger welled up inside Sarah to see her three pets relegated to a life in the kennels: for a moment she forgot to be grateful to discover that they were still alive. Bubbles Kamir, the lively scarred lurcher, lean and energetic and bounding everywhere; the more sedate Princess, an elderly afghan hound who had been badly mistreated by her first owners; and trotting after them as fast as his stubby white legs would carry him, little Scottie the scots terrier who had appeared from nowhere one night and had decided of his own accord to stay.

As Sarah watched them race along the path to the beach, she began to understand that Kath Brown could not at first have afforded to keep those three dogs loose about the house as Sarah had done, because she was not Sarah. The lurcher would have defended Sarah's property from her, the scottie would have strayed again, and Princess would have cowered from her: the reactions of any one of the dogs would have given Kath Brown away to someone like her employer Neil Davison. Sarah brought her anger back under control and once again asked God to speak and act through her and to control the outcome of the meeting.

Smith touched her arm and nodded to her to go. Her apprehension melted away. In the power of God's strength she stood up and walked out from between the dunes onto the beach.

CHAPTER 26

The sea air was tangy and salt upon her tongue. To her left lay the firth with the misty hills of the northern kingdom beyond. To her right lay the dunes and the rising sun, and Smith and his company on guard out of sight. Her footfalls were noiseless on the damp flat sand. Her ears were filled with the roll of the waves on the shore at low tide, the mewing of the gulls as they wheeled in the blue sky above, the rush of the breeze as it fanned her hair, and the rush of her breath through her nostrils. She could feel every muscle in her body, so heightened was her awareness. She moved to the pulse of her heart and the press of her lungs. She looked down from above and watched herself walking along, surrounded by the encouragement of the communion of saints; the golden helix spinning so quickly in the light of truth that it was becoming invisible in the blue-white light of God beyond.

Ahead, unaware, strolled the woman she had come to meet, with her two Alsatians pulling energetically on their leashes, accompanied by the three other dogs who wove round about them.

Suddenly the lurcher dog stopped and turned, his ears pricked. He recognised his mistress at once and bounded towards her, whimpering with joy as she called his name, laughing and almost crying to see him again. He leapt up into her arms and licked her face, his tail wagging enough nearly to unbalance him. Behind him bounded the little scottie dog as if on springs, his stubby legs struggling to keep up; and after them strode Princess, her joints arthritic and stiff in old age.

Kath Brown turned to see what had attracted the three dogs to move away. Her right arm was pulled to one side by the two restrained Alsatians as they barked at the stranger on the shore.

To Kath Sarah was no stranger. She stared at her, at first bewildered, then in shock.

'You?' she gasped: 'You should be dead.'

Sarah gazed at Kath's fearful expression and felt the last of her own anger, resentment, contempt and fear for her dissolve away. She pitied her. She even felt compassion for this pathetic woman whose past was about to catch up with her so fatefully.

'Is that what you arranged for me, Kath? Death?' she asked.

She spoke without recrimination and only asked to hear the truth; but truth itself was recrimination to Kath Brown. She shied away from the question and the questioner to walk on northwards along the wide flat beach. Sarah chased after her to hear her answer.

'No, only that we wouldn't see you again. Darren was the one who handled that side of things – he was clever that way. I did all the donkey work, you know: took the pictures, made myself a name, entered the exhibitions and won the advertising contracts. I really was a good photographer, you know. I could photograph anything anywhere; and whenever I had to I could even develop all my own films.'

Even the way Kath spoke sounded pathetic to Sarah, who pitied the talented young woman for her lack of confidence in her ability; until she realised that Kath was merely trying to put the blame on someone else again.

'While your brother handled all the rest, all the less legitimate things,' Sarah prompted.

'All Darren did was to cash in on golden opportunities. We never touched anything that wasn't handed to us on a plate.'

Sarah looked down at the glistening sand, saddened to hear the excuses which she knew were to convince Katherine rather than herself of her own basic integrity. Katherine could not face up to her faults. Sarah chose not to challenge her excuses yet because she did not want to put her on the defensive so soon. She strolled on along the beach with Kath on her left side, in the manner of a friend who is willing to be a confidante. After Kath had fought her conscience alone for three years, Sarah sensed she would need a confidante.

'And where is your brother now?' she asked.

Kath caught her breath. Even to think that answer made her feel her vulnerability without him.

'Darren's dead,' she said. 'He was in the capital on business the morning the bombs struck, staying at a hotel....'

Sarah's mind flew back to that strange hotel lobby the day after she had returned, and the plastic resident dressed in clothes she recognised who had tapped her shoulder three times and warned her to get out of the building before it collapsed.

'Room number X15, the hotel by the park,' she remembered. 'Yes, I saw Darren there, in the hotel I stayed in when I first got back.'

'You've been back that long?' Kath demanded in astonishment. 'He didn't mention seeing you.'

'He wouldn't have. It was less than two weeks ago. He'd been dead for over two years.'

Kath walked on in silence, understanding what Sarah had just said in terms of physical remains rather than psychic perception. Sarah watched her with a pitying smile as her head moved from side to side in indecision. John Smith's lecture about time running out, and her own thoughts about the survivors being the most successful people, gained new significance in the light of Darren Brown's death.

'You weren't political agents at all, were you, Kath? - you were just industrial spies. What was it that got you both so far out of your depth? Blackmail?'

Kath turned on her in protest, her eyes blazing.

'You know already, don't you! You've no need to ask these questions: you already have the answers. You're just trying to make me incriminate myself.'

'With what witnesses? Five dogs? Kath, I've been away a long time. I made a lot of stupid mistakes for which I've paid the price and now I just want to go home. For three years I've yearned for my quiet little life again. All I want to do now is go back to living here by the sea, caring for all those unwanted animals, painting all my unwanted pictures, and practising what many once thought an unwanted faith. So it was blackmail.'

'Yes,' Kath admitted: 'It was.'

She stopped to look across the sea at the hills of the northern kingdom as she wondered what to do about this persistent woman who had returned to take back her rightful place. Sarah sensed what Kath was thinking and watched in alarm as she unleashed the Alsatians, unable to warn her that if the two dogs went for her they would be shot. To her relief the Alsatians briefly turned their heads towards her in amiable curiosity and then bounded off into the sea. Princess, Scottie and Bubbles Kamir all followed, but none of them went far enough to get their paws wet. Scottie chased after the waves and ran from them yapping in playful anger.

'We were discovered taking pictures in the wrong part of a factory. I hadn't realised it, but Darren had asked me to photograph some electronic blueprints for a top secret allied defence contract, not a commercial system at all. An agent from the allied forces quickly moved in. We could be prosecuted and have our careers ruined, or we could do the allies a favour and smuggle some information over to the other side. Which option would anyone take? Of course we said yes; as long as the information was in a form we used in our work, we'd take anything anywhere. Six months later ten of us went on our minibus tour, with you in the vacant place at the last minute. How you never wondered why we should take that sort of holiday on our income, I'll never know.'

Sarah shrugged her shoulders.

'I simply presumed your sort of photography was expensive, or that you enjoyed the camaraderie of the trekking life. So it was no accident I ended up on that tour.'

Kath shook her head.

'No. We made it seem like that to you and the others. Then

later, when we gave our account to the authorities, we made it seem like you had forced Marcia into being unable to go.'

'But you weren't to know I'd smuggle Bibles.'

Kath laughed and kicked meaninglessly at a piece of seaweed washed up on the sand.

'Of course we knew you would! We suggested the idea to you through Café Annie. She knew just how to get you to take the bait. You were so very idealistic then, and still far too immature to be cautious. How you puffed up with self-importance for doing your bit to save the world! And broke too. You were a real pain! We only put up with you 'cause you were the….'

She faltered as she realised what the confession must be sounding like to the woman at her side, but regained confidence when she considered that they were alone on the beach and her two Alsatians would be more than a match for Sarah's three strays. She continued:

'We only tolerated you because you and I looked enough alike for us to change places during the arrest.'

Sarah pulled a brief one-sided smile to hear Kath's shame at speaking about what she had not thought shame to commit.

'You don't need to choose your words for me, Kath: I leave vengeance to God,' she reassured. 'Indeed, I have no reason to be resentful towards you, for through your betrayal I was safely well away from all the bombing. Had you and I not changed places, I might have gone the same way as your brother.'

Kath had not expected that reaction from Sarah. She checked Sarah's facial expression to make sure it matched the sentiments she had expressed, and began to envisage a way to escape the just reward for her own duplicity. If Sarah really was going to be so reasonable about the whole thing, perhaps she could be persuaded to let things stay as Kath had made them. Kath tested her cautiously, putting on a nervous air.

'Then why this big scene, Sarah? Why not just turf me out and denounce me?'

'I simply want to know the truth, before I start out on my new life. You know, why it happened, how it happened, see if I need to pray for you, so that I can find forgiveness myself. You and Darren were very clever, and your performances were faultless. I never guessed that you were both acting.'

Kath called the Alsatians to draw their attention as she turned to stroll south along the beach. In doing so, she casually placed Sarah between herself and the dunes, making them walk closer to the dogs and the sea. Sarah found herself forced to walk right beside Kath to hear her soft voice against the roll of the waves over the beach. She wondered whether Smith was picking up anything at all of their conversation and Kath Brown's confession, and feared that because Kath suspected an eavesdropper she was deliberately making them walk closer to the water's edge.

'I hawked your Bibles for you on the other side,' Kath continued. 'I had had some previous experience of the black market and knew just how to get caught. And Darren persuaded you to take those dramatic shots in black and white with one of my cameras, remember? You were struck by the configuration of walls and trees, after I had pointed it out to you – the artist's eye! A pity tourists weren't permitted to take photos there! You didn't suspect a thing. We moulded you like clay in our hands.'

Still Sarah did not take offence at the insults Kath was hurling at her. Her patience told Kath that Sarah would indeed be willing to negotiate an acceptable solution to their identity problems for them both; and if truth was the price, it was a small enough price to pay for that.

'So you got us both arrested, Kath,' Sarah prompted gently.

Kath nodded.

'You were knocked out during our arrest. I had all the say. I explained about the Bible you got me to give you, the way you cut out a section inside it to make a secret compartment, and I told them that you were a photographer by profession. I confessed about myself, that I was a naïve Christian, a farmhand who stupidly tried a bit of smuggling. They questioned you, you denied that, claimed it was the other way round. They looked at the Bible, found the package inside it with your fingerprints on; and concluded that you were the sinister spy, willing to sell to any government or individual the secrets you purloined wherever you went. The compartment contained photos of an allied navigation device, a homeland code, background information about an allied nuclear strike from the homeland, and the pictures you were taking of some of the targets of that strike. They thought you were a highly trained professional international special agent. The tried to break you. Because you were innocent of their accusations you couldn't be broken; so you should have died.'

Bubbles Kamir raced off across the sand towards the dunes, swift and graceful as a young deer. Sarah called his name and whistled a command which brought him circling back, his ears pricked up and his head turned towards her. She casually changed direction and strolled towards him diagonally away from the sea. Kath followed unthinkingly, hastened a little by the Alsatians who came racing out of the water and showered her as they shook themselves dry. She scolded them affectionately and ducked away laughing as they boisterously leapt up to give her friendly wet hugs in return.

'This is why I tend to keep Sunda and Kaido on leads on the beach,' she explained to Sarah.

With Kath's experienced handling the two Alsatians soon calmed down. She rejoined Sarah about half-way across the beach between the sea and the dunes. They continued their conversation and their early morning stroll.

'And you?' Sarah prompted at length: 'You were charged with attempting to smuggle goods into the country, I suppose.'

'Yes. It was the intent more than the contraband that I was done for.'

'Really? Not rather that they doubted your story and convicted you on a minor charge so that they could hold you until they found out the truth and made a deal with you? After all, it was you, not I, who told them where the bogus information was hidden. You set our homeland up that day, Kath, not just me; and Doug Chandler was in on the deal.'

'That's not true!' Kath protested: 'The allies set it up, not Doug or me. I was only the messenger boy, and you were my fall guy.'

Sarah sadly shook her head. Kath's protest told her that Kath's confidence in the rightness of her actions was fading. Though Kath's self-satisfied recitation of facts and motives was not a real confession, they would satisfy John Smith as her admission of guilt. But Sarah still wanted to go on, to force Kath into a truer confession. Sooner or later Kath would have to account for her duplicity, whether under duress to John Smith or as she entered eternity. Sarah believed it was better for her to walk through the trauma there and then while she could still repent and while she had a confessor who loved her as a fellow creature of God despite all that she had done.

'Even the way you speak betrays you, Kath,' she said. 'The verification of detail means little to me, though it seems to mean so much to you. Three years on and you're still so precise about the details that whether they're facts or excuses, all I hear is self-justification, which indicates only guilt. The automatic defence – "No, of course I wasn't wrong". We're all human, Kath. To hear the way you talk about me to my face as if you're so clever and I'm so stupid, tells me how human you are, how guilty you feel, and how sick you must be to think your victim would accept such criticism without a murmur.

'Before you level anything more at me, maybe you should remember this. I'm still here, and I've done my time: I have the rest of my natural life ahead of me to spend as I will in freedom. But clever Darren is dead; and you live in fear, maybe not every moment now but still every day, every time a stranger knocks at the door or a new voice speaks behind you. So tell me, who's the stupid one now?'

Kath was shocked by Sarah's unexpected attack and her understanding of her present situation. Too surprised to protest, she gaped vacantly while Sarah continued her forceful response.

'Do you think there weren't moments after I got back and saw all the devastation in the cities, when I asked myself, "Kath Brown, how could you have done this? What could possibly have persuaded you to destroy so many lives?" Like the factory I sheltered in, the piles of dust and the clothes still at the machines the hands were working the moment the bombs struck. Like the last assembly at my old school, the rows upon rows of little uniforms on the hall floor. Like my mother at her desk, her handbag open; my father at their house, still decomposing in a virtually sealed room. And then there are the living dead: the man of God, his face half cindered, who only lasted two years on; the woman in the café whose whole existence is tears in a cup of cold tea; the insane, who witnessed the destruction of their families and their lives and escaped into a living death. And I had six crucial months missing out of my life. So I asked myself, "Am I really responsible for all this?" And I could say with a clear conscience, "Thank God in God's mercy I'm not!"'

'Shut up!' Kath suddenly shouted.

'Why should I, Katherine Brown? You never spared a thought for me. You never spared a thought for the people you condemned to death or to a living hell. You never spared a thought for Darren....'

'No! It wasn't like that!' she screamed. 'It wasn't my choice. We were only one tiny part of a far more massive plot. If we hadn't done it, they'd only have got someone else to do it instead, and my career would have been ruined. You do see, don't you.'

'Yes, I see. Isn't your career ruined now?'

Three soldiers walked out from between the dunes. Two were carrying rifles, Smith the third between them holding a revolver. Kath paled and turned on Sarah in venomous hatred.

'You lied to me!'

She threw herself at Sarah, her hands gripping her throat to throttle her. The dogs all turned, bristling. The two Alsatians leapt into attack to help their mistress. They fell lifeless in the sand, three shots in each.

Kath pulled Sarah across her body to shield herself against the soldiers' next shots, her hands tightening around her throat. Unable to help Sarah while she was shielding Kath, Smith signalled to the men in the dunes not to fire, and ordered the two beside him to move cautiously in with him. With the outcome of the fight in the balance, he could only hope on the result going to Sarah's recent prison discipline rather than Kath's fear and desperation.

Sarah pulled ineffectively at Kath's arms as her grip tightened further around her neck. Kath dragged her further back, trying to keep her distance from the armed men.

Bubbles Kamir leapt in. He snapped at Kath to make her release his long lost mistress, growling to intimidate her. When she ignored him, he bit savagely at her arms and body. Princess joined in, worrying the bodies of the Alsatians to make sure they would not fight on; and Scottie hopped on his hind legs on the sidelines, yapping noisily to add his voice to the fray. Despite their support, Kath maintained her stranglehold and Sarah continued to weaken. Her feeble punches had no effect on Kath and her legs began to give way.

Bubbles Kamir clamped his jaws firmly round Kath's right ankle. She cried out in sudden agony as he crushed the bones between his teeth. Unbalanced, she fell to the sand, pulling Sarah down with her. The jolt on landing made her release her grip. Sarah quickly threw herself out of her reach and rolled back over onto her knees, gasping for breath.

With his prey down, Bubbles Kamir went for Kath's throat, growling deeply. She screamed.

'Hold, Bubbles, hold!' Sarah ordered in a hoarse voice before he could do any more damage.

The lurcher froze, still growling, his jaws clamped round

Kath's neck, his teeth pressing into her skin but not yet crushing her. When Kath tried to pull away, he growled more deeply and adjusted his bite to hold her more firmly. She stopped fighting against him.

'Please, call the dog off,' Kath cried, her voice half strangled, her chest heaving with the pain from her ankle and her fear of the dog at her throat.

Sarah shook her head and rubbed her own aching neck.

'Not yet. You still have your price to pay,' she said.

'But Christians are meant to show mercy,' Kath protested fearfully. '… if you are a Christian!'

'Why should I show you any more mercy than you showed me? We will both be answerable to the same Higher Power after our lives' end. Pay the price in this world and repent. Then you may be saved from suffering in the next.'

'You're insane! This dog is killing me, and you're just letting him.'

'Stop trying me, Katherine. Don't mistake meekness for weakness, and don't confuse weakness with love.'

John Smith came between them, the two soldiers on either side. Kath saw their uniforms and cried tears of relief as she spotted the insignia of Smith's rank.

'Thank God you're here, Major' she croaked. 'Help, get this dog off me and arrest that woman. She claims to be me, but she's really Katherine Ella Brown, the famous photographer and an international spy.'

Smith scowled at her in contempt and gave a short harsh laugh.

'It won't work this time, Katherine Brown. We heard everything you and Sarah said. Show her the transmitter, Sarah. And call off your dog before he does some real damage.'

Sarah ordered Bubbles Kamir to let go and come to her. The lurcher obeyed at once. As he sprang back the two soldiers stepped in to cover Kath with their rifles. She sat up to nurse her injured ankle and massage her sore neck.

Sarah took Smith's transmitter out of her pocket and threw it at Kath. Out of another pocket she brought a small voice recorder which she handed back to Smith.

'Now you will begin to know how it felt for me to be set up,' Sarah coldly told Kath.

'With rather more justification!' Smith said.

His tone turned to pure contempt as he ordered his men to take Kath away. They lifted her onto her feet and half-carried her when they found her crushed ankle could not bear her weight.

Smith helped Sarah to stand but watched Kath leave with his men before he turned to talk to her one last time.

'We could hardly make out a word,' he admitted. 'We won't have any of her confession on record until the backroom boys get to work on the recording and cut out all the interference from the waves and the gulls and I don't know what else.'

'Then how did you know to step in when you did?'

'We did hear most of the last bit, after you managed to lead her away from the sea and straight towards our pickup. But I knew long before then that you would be going free today.'

'How? If you couldn't hear anything....'

'I knew the moment your lurcher sensed your presence and ran to greet you. I knew as soon as you shouted to Bubbles to Kamir. You have a very well-trained dog there, Sarah Baylis.'

'Just a well loved one.'

She crouched down beside the scarred lurcher to rub his short-haired coat affectionately. Princess and Scottie pushed their way in too, not wanting to be left out of the greeting. She kissed their noses and looked back up at Smith.

'Now that you know for certain who I am, Mr X, would you mind telling me your real name, so that I can thank you properly? It seems unfair not to redress the balance.'

He restrained himself to one laugh alone.

'Didn't your sixth sense tell you, Sarah? You've been calling me by the right name all along. Jonathan Edwin Smith at your service, Ma'am,' he said, with a little bow and an enigmatic smile which left her convinced that she still did not know his true identity.

He looked at her more seriously and continued, 'You know, you were quite professional there with her, played the line and hooked her as neatly as you liked. Have you ever thought of joining a team like ours? You seem to have all the basic qualities we look for.'

She stood up and scowled at him. At once Bubbles Kamir was standing in front of her growling at him to warn him off.

'While I must thank you for saving me, John Smith, I would never ever dream of joining your team. No true follower of Jesus Christ would ever think of doing to another creature what your men are about to do to Kath Brown. Don't make retribution revenge – no matter what you do to her, you will not bring back one alive of all those dead; you will not turn the clock back one minute, or make anything like it was before again.'

She paused to reassure Bubbles Kamir by patting his tense shoulders.

'Perhaps it is harder for those like you who were left behind, who had to wait and watch while all the things they held dear were taken from them,' she said. 'It is easier when you've risked your life and won, to cut your losses and lay new foundations to start building again. The time for trying to make the old way work ended the moment they let fly the first bomb.'

She turned and tried to walk away. He caught hold of her right arm to stop her. She shook him off impatiently.

'No, John. I cannot stop you doing whatever you will to the owner of those two dead Alsatians lying over there, but don't expect me to condone it. There is no place for vengeance in my world. If you find you've tired of it too, drop me a line: you know my address. If not, you go your way; and I'll go mine.'

She turned once more and walked away, spreading out her arms to embrace the long-missed landscape whose voice she could hear welcoming her home. He watched her go, knowing instinctively that now she would go back to her painting, and be a success; that now she would go back to her church and be a catalyst for reform; that now she would re-enter society and take enough part in it to ensure the greater good. And he, if he survived, would become no more than another retired army major ready to take down all the road signs whenever there was a threat of war.

The tide was turning, and the three joyful dogs were herding her back home. He watched her silhouette pass on into the morning, a slender black outline against the sun on the silver path reflected across the glistening sands.

THE END

www.ingramcontent.com/pod-product-compliance
Lightning Source LLC
Chambersburg PA
CBHW070459260626
47161CB00004B/1374